THE
FLOODS
6

The Great Outdoors

THE FLOODS

6
The Great Outdoors

Colin Thompson

illustrations by the author

RANDOM HOUSE AUSTRALIA

This work is fictitious. Any resemblance to anyone living or dead is purely coincidental. If you think one of the characters in this book is like you, then you are very lucky, but remember, it's not nice to boast.

A Random House book
Published by Random House Australia Pty Ltd
Level 3, 100 Pacific Highway, North Sydney, NSW 2060
www.randomhouse.com.au

First published by Random House in 2008

Addresses for companies within the Random House Group can be found at www.randomhouse.com.au/offices.

National Library of Australia
Cataloguing-in-Publication Entry

Thompson, Colin (Colin Edward).
The great outdoors.

For primary school age.
ISBN 978 174166 253 5 (pbk.).

I. Title. (Series: Thompson, Colin (Colin Edward) Floods; 6).

A823.3

Design, illustrations and typesetting by Colin Thompson
Additional typesetting by Anna Warren, Warren Ventures
Printed and bound by Griffin Press, South Australia

Random House Australia uses papers that are natural, renewable and recyclable products and made from wood grown in sustainable forests. The logging and manufacturing processes are expected to conform to the environmental regulations of the country of origin.

10 9 8 7 6 5 4 3 2 1

The Floods' Family Tree

MERLIN ♥ **MORDONNA**
Wizard   Witch

Valla
Boy - 23

Satanella
Girl - 17

Merlinmary
Not sure - 16

Winchflat
Boy - 15

Morbid & Silent
Twin boys - 11*

Betty
Girl - 11

* The twins decided to stay 11 years old for three years so they are now the same age as Betty. Next year, on their 12th birthday, they will turn 14.

For Charlie

1995–2008

Who was Ruby and Rosie and several other
dogs all at the same time, especially Satanella
even though he was a boy.

PLEASE NOTE: No Belgian people were harmed
in the making of this book, though several were
given moustaches to protect their identity.*

** But only the women. The men were given magic When-You-
Look-At-Me-You-Will-Think-I-Am-Someone-Completely-
Different socks.*

PROLOGUE

For those of you who haven't already read ANY of the FIVE earlier books:

Blah, di blah, di blah, di blah and blah and lah, di da, di blah, di blah di blah. Blah, di blah, di blah, di blah and blah and lah, di da, di blah, di blah di blah. Blah, di blah, di blah, di blah and blah and lah, di da, di blah, di blah di blah. Blah, di blah, di blah, di blah and blah and lah, di da, di blah, di blah di blah. Blah, di blah, di blah, di blah and blah and lah, di da, di blah, di blah di blah. Blah, di blah, di blah, di blah and blah and lah, di da, di blah, di blah di blah.

What, you think I'm going to waste pages and pages writing a summary of, like, five whole books? Just go and get them yourself and read them . . .

If you have already read the other books, you are very clever and welcome back.

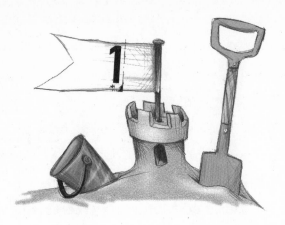

After months of surfing the net, looking at hundreds of magazines and watching dozens of TV travel shows, the Floods had finally booked to go on holiday.

Although Mordonna and Nerlin had sailed around the world when they had eloped from Transylvania Waters, they had never been to the seaside in the way you go to the seaside on holiday, to swim and make sandcastles and lie around getting sunburnt.

When the idea of a holiday had first been suggested, Winchflat Flood had said they should

probably rent a nice remote house somewhere so no one would bother them.

'What you mean,' said Betty, 'is so we don't bother anyone else.'

'Well, yes, I suppose so,' Winchflat admitted. 'I mean, we don't exactly look like your average human family, do we?'

'It's true,' said Mordonna. 'People do tend to cross the road when we approach and small babies and dogs cry a lot when they see us.'

Mordonna was preparing the dinner as she spoke. She was knitting several very long worms together to make Wizard Wraps, which were then stuffed with Hot 'N' Spicy Chilli Warts that she herself had collected from the armpits of a family of hippos at the local zoo.[1]

'So we should look for a quiet house all on its own next to a nice beach,' said Nerlin, who was meant to be peeling potatoes at the kitchen sink

---

[1] *Actually, that could be a typing mistake. Mordonna could have collected the warts from the armpits of a family of hippies at the local zoo.*

but kept peeling the ends of his fingers.

'No,' said Mordonna. 'I want to stay in a posh hotel where someone opens the door for you and they iron your socks and put chocolates on your pillow every night when they turn down your bed.'

'But I put chocolates on your bed every night already,' said Nerlin.

'I know, but you always give me the hard ones with the toffee because *you* eat all the nice ones,' said Mordonna. 'No, I want to stay in a big posh seaside hotel with a big posh name like the Grande or the Splendide, where we won't have to do the washing up and there aren't spiders living under the beds.'

'You mean we'll have to take our own spiders?' said one of the twins.[2]

Morbid and Silent were sitting under the kitchen table catching the worms that kept wriggling off Mordonna's chopping board. For

---

[2] *As you already know, only one of the twins, Morbid and Silent, speaks and I can't remember whose turn it is.*

every five they caught they gave four back to their mother and took it in turns eating the fifth one.

'I doubt it,' said Satanella. 'I expect really posh hotels have a choice of spiders. They might even have scorpions and cockroaches.'

'They don't mention them on their websites,' said Winchflat. 'And humans are frightened of spiders.'

'Frightened of spiders?' said Satanella, picking another one out of the family snack bowl that lived

next to the toaster.[3] 'How can anyone be frightened of spiders? They're delicious.'

'It's just another one of those things that make humans so weird,' said Mordonna.

Mordonna and Nerlin Flood and their seven children were not going on holiday on their own. Their friends, the Hulberts, who lived three doors away at number 19 Acacia Avenue, were going with them. The Hulberts were most definitely not witches or wizards. They were very, very ordinary, extra-normal human beings. There was Mr and Mrs Hulbert, their daughter, Ffiona, who was Betty's best friend, and Ffiona's little brother, Claude, who was in love with Satanella and still at the age where eating earth seemed like a really good idea.[4]

---

[3] *You don't want to know what the toaster was used for. Actually, if you are reading this book you probably do want to know, but because of new sustainable environmental rules put in place by the government, I'm not allowed to tell you.*

[4] *Witches and wizards like to eat a bit of earth whatever age they are – unlike humans, who usually grow out of it by the age of three, unless they join the Ancient Order of Earth Eaters, a strange Belgian offshoot of the Masons.*

The Floods thought that surely the Hulberts, being human, would know all about the sort of things you do on holiday and be able to explain what was so good about sitting on a beach getting sand in all your cracks and creases.

But Mr and Mrs Hulbert, who were both forty-seven, had never once been to the seaside, not even for a day out as children. Trips to the seaside were fun, and neither Mr nor Mrs Hulbert's parents did that sort of thing. To them fun was a sin that always ended in tears. They thought that looking at postcards of the seaside could make the blood rush to your head. They had never even stayed in a hotel.

'Those sort of places are not for the likes of us,' Mrs Hulbert's father had said when his daughter had asked about them.

'Of course not,' said Mrs Hulbert's mother. 'They are places of sin and wickedness. Now eat your cabbage soup and go and polish your shoes and make sure all your hair pins are pointing in the same direction. Oh dear, but it's rude to point – I

meant to say make sure they're *lying* in the same direction . . . but then it's wrong to lie, too. So, I mean, well, you know perfectly well what I mean, my girl.'

Mr Hulbert's parents had been the same, so it was hardly surprising that the two of them had grown up very timid and old-fashioned. However, since they had met the Floods their lives had changed. Most people would be scared of a family of wizards, but with Mordonna and Betty's guidance and encouragement, plus some added magic, the Hulberts had realised that they too could have a life.

Gradually they had become more laid-back. Mrs Hulbert often took the twenty-four hair pins out of her long brown hair and let it hang down over her shoulders, and in the past month Mr Hulbert had spent one hundred and ninety-three hours not wearing a tie.[5]

So they weren't a lot of help when it came to

---

[5] *Next month he is hoping to pass two hundred hours.*

finding out about going away on holiday.

'I saw a programme about holidays on the television,' said Mrs Hulbert. 'There was lots of sunshine and people talking in foreign languages and people who were wearing really tiny clothes and lying down in the middle of the day on flat bits of sand by water and then eating strange-looking food in loud noisy places at night.'

'Bikinis, mother,' said Ffiona. 'They're called bikinis.'

'Well, I don't care what they're called, I don't think *I* want to eat any.'

'No, no,' Ffiona started to explain. 'Oh, never mind.'

'I like the sound of the strange-looking food,' said Satanella. 'Was there gristle and moving bits?'

'Maybe we could get a book,' Winchflat suggested. 'Something like *Going On Holiday for Dummies*.'

But they could not find a single book about how to go on holiday.

'I suppose humans are born with the

information inside their brains, like birds migrating to warm places for the winter,' said Nerlin.

'We weren't,' said Ffiona.

'Well, that's probably because we already live in a warm place,' said Betty.

So in the end they decided they would have a rehearsal. They looked through magazines and holiday brochures and watched a TV series about hotels called *Fawlty Towers*. Then they made some of the cellars under 11 Acacia Avenue look like the inside of a hotel and they took it in turns to work in the hotel and be the guests. Of course, they hadn't realised that *Fawlty Towers* was a comedy series and that most hotels are not run by people who are crazy.

'Are you sure you want to go on holiday?' said Nerlin after a week where they had all taken it in turns being rude to each other and eating yesterday's leftovers with carrots that had been boiled to mush.

Then they went down to the deepest cellars and made a fake seaside with a beach and waves and

deckchairs and sandcastles, but because they were almost forty metres below ground level, no amount of magic could make the sun shine and they all turned blue and got nasty colds. This meant they had to take spoonfuls of Old Retchup's Cure-All, which was actually far worse than any illness it was meant to cure.[6]

---

6   *See the back of the book for more information on this and other Old Retchup's products.*

'I think we're probably not doing this holiday thing right,' said Mrs Hulbert. 'I'm sure you're supposed to enjoy yourself. I think that's why people have holidays.'

'Yes, and also, you know what they say,' Mr Hulbert added, 'a change is as good as a rest.'

'Oh, I don't agree with that,' said Nerlin. 'I changed into a toad once and I didn't enjoy it nearly as much as having a nice lie-down.'

'Yes, but don't forget the time you changed into a feather duster,' said Mordonna. 'You enjoyed that, didn't you? I know I did.'

'True.'

'No, no,' said Mrs Hulbert. 'I think it means a change of scene is as good as a rest.'

'Seen? Seen what?' said Nerlin.

'I think I'll go on that internet thing and just book us all a holiday somewhere nice,' said Mordonna.

'There are a couple of things we have to do before we leave,' said Mordonna after she had booked their holiday and the Hulberts had gone home to pack. 'First of all, I need volunteers to go out and dig up Granny. We can't possibly go on holiday without her.'

You might think that no one would offer to dig up a dead body, but the children loved their granny and they all rushed out into the garden and began digging. Of course, being a dog, Satanella usually did all the digging, but when it was Dead-Granny-Digging-Up, everyone insisted on a turn.

'Be careful, children,' Mordonna called after them. 'Granny might be asleep and you know how bits of her can fall off if she gets a sudden shock.'

Since Queen Scratchrot had been buried, quite a few bits of her had fallen off, even without her getting a shock. At first Mordonna had kept them all in a box under the kitchen sink, but then Winchflat had built a special Dead-Granny-Backpack and all the fallen-off bits were kept in its special mould-proof zip-up pockets.[7] At some point in the future the family planned to stick all the bits back together again with the famous Doctor Julian Frankenstein's Amazing Incredible Two-Pack, Low-Fat Corpse Adhesive,[8] but for the moment the Queen was quite happy as she was.

'I like travelling light,' she said.

The Dead-Granny-Backpack proved to be extra useful now that the Queen was being dug up to accompany the family on holidays. The

---

[7] *See the back of the book for information on how to get your very own Dead-Granny-Backpack.*

[8] *As used in* The Floods 5: Prime Suspect.

children lifted her out of her coffin and folded her up inside the main part of the backpack with her head sticking out of the top so she could see what was going on with her one remaining eye.[9]

'Oh, how lovely,' said the Queen when the children told her their plans. 'I haven't been on holiday for years. Last time I went it was before I met your grandfather. My parents took me to the Great Exhibition in London in 1851. We went on the opening day and because we were royalty, we met Queen Victoria. Prince Albert even kissed me on the cheek. Not this cheek,' she added, pointing to the left side of her face, 'the one in the plastic bag in that pocket down there.'

'Well, this time, Granny,' said Betty, 'we're going to the seaside.'

'I'll need some new clothes,' said the Queen. 'A nice sarong and one of those bikini things.'

'Euggh, Granny, I don't think so,' said Betty.

---

[9] *Her other eye was in one of the zip-up pockets, where it was 'keeping an eye' on her other fallen-off bits.*

'Of course,' said the Queen with a chuckle, 'I could always go topless.'

'Ohh, Granny.'

'Well, considering most of my skin has fallen off, I'm topless already,' said the Queen and she laughed so much that her left knee shot out of the backpack and across the room.

'One thing's for sure,' she said as tears of laughter rolled down her one remaining cheek into her shoulder socket, 'I won't need any sunscreen.'

At this the entire family fell about in hysterics.

'You are the best granny in the whole world,' said Betty as she finished painting the Queen's seven remaining fingernails with her favourite Rhesus Red nail varnish.

'And you are the prettiest granddaughter,' said the Queen.

'Do you want to bring Igorina, darling?' Mordonna asked Winchflat.

Igorina was the girlfriend that Winchflat had built himself. Although everyone called her

his girlfriend, they had never been out on a date together or even kissed each other and the only time Winchflat had held her hand was before he had joined it onto the rest of her body. She was not so much a girlfriend as a zombie, but with less charm and beauty. Winchflat thought of her more like a backup girlfriend in case he couldn't find a proper one.

'I don't think so, Mother,' he said. 'Apart from the fact that she has terrible table manners,[10] she looks so freaky that she scares everyone who sees her, including me.'

'If you're sure, darling,' said Mordonna, feeling very relieved.

Being a witch and having grown up in Transylvania Waters, Mordonna had seen many weird and terrifying creatures, so the sight of Igorina didn't faze her at all. It was the smell.[11] The thought of spending time cooped up with that terrible smell in the shiny red minibus that Mr Hulbert had hired for the week was almost enough to make her cancel the whole holiday.

Before they left, Mordonna called Parsnip

---

[10] *Instead of eating off tables like everyone else, Igorina actually tries to eat the table. You can read more about Igorina in* The Floods 4: Survivor.

[11] *Take the fifteen worst smells you can think of – and really use your grossest imagination. Multiply each one by fifty, add them all together and then stick your nose into the middle of it and sniff as hard as you can. This will make you throw up, which will actually make it smell nicer. Igorina smells worse.*

down from the roof. Parsnip was a Transylvanian Crow who belonged to Queen Scratchrot's devoted manservant, Vessel, who the Hearse Whisperer, an evil spy who worked for Mordonna's father, the King of Transylvania Waters, had trapped in an enchanted birdcage in an attempt to lure Mordonna out of hiding so she could take her back to the King.[12]

'Parsnip, my good and faithful bird,' said Mordonna.

'Uh oh, bad stuff coming now,' said Parsnip. 'Nice speak always bring bad stuff, Snip-Snip know that.'

'No, really,' said Mordonna. 'All I want to say is that we're going on holiday and we'd like you to keep an eye on things back here.'

'Snip-Snip need holiday,' said Parsnip.

---

[12] *This paragraph will only seem incredibly complicated if you have not read* The Floods 3: Home & Away *– and if you have read it, you already know who Parsnip is so you won't have to read the convoluted paragraph. However, if you hadn't read it, then you wouldn't be reading this footnote. Complicated, isn't it?*

'Well, when we get back, then you can go on holiday yourself,' said Mordonna. 'You could go and visit all your friends.'

'Snip-Snip only got one friend and he trapped in enchanted birdcage,' said Parsnip. 'And you said Snip-Snip not to go see him or Worse Hisperer will get you.'

'Well, where do other crows go on their holidays?'

'Not have holidays,' said Parsnip. 'Just hang around and eat dead things.'

'Well then,' said Mordonna. 'When we get back, you can go off and do that. In the meantime, though, I really need you to look after everything here.'

Parsnip said that he wanted to go to the seaside with them and eat different dead things – the kind of dead things that you only get at the seaside, like slimy fish and bits of decaying lobster. Mordonna said she would bring him some back, but he still wasn't happy.

'Look, it's a very important job staying here,' Mordonna said. 'And when we come back I'll bring you a big surprise.'

'What is it?'

'You'll have to wait and see. It's a surprise.'

'You just speaking that,' Parsnip said. He flew back up to the roof to attack some pigeons and make himself feel better.

He could see that Mordonna had that 'if-I-have-any-more-trouble-from-you-I'll-turn-you-into-something-small-and-slimy' look in her eye.

Least Snip-Snip not have to helping washing out hang for two weekly, he thought. *Beak pretending be clothes peg is making jaw sore, so good rest have.*

Parsnip thought they were only leaving him behind because he was just a crow and they didn't

23

really like him, but he was wrong. In the back of Mordonna's mind there was always the fear that one of the King's spies would finally track them down. If this happened while they were away, then Parsnip would be able to fly down and warn them.

She knew her fears were probably unfounded. After all, they had imprisoned the King's most dangerous spy, the Hearse Whisperer, in a sealed magic bottle buried at the bottom of the deepest part of the ocean, the Mariana Trench.[13]

But, she thought, *you can never be too careful.* How right she was.[14]

---

[13] *See* The Floods 5: Prime Suspect.

[14] *This footnote is not here to give you a clue about what might, or might not, happen in the future. It's just here to make you feel uneasy.*

24

The place that Mordonna had chosen for their holiday was perfect: a peaceful little town by the sea called Port Folio. There was a harbour with picturesque fishing boats and lovely old buildings all along the waterfront, and further along there were miles of golden sand and bright blue sea. It was the sort of place that had probably looked exactly the same for the past hundred years. A lot of the people there certainly looked as if they had been there for a hundred years. It was also the sort of place where the Floods would probably cause very little comment because most of the population walked

around looking at their feet, so they wouldn't notice them. And if people did notice that the visitors were rather strange, they would be far too polite to say anything.

Their journey to Port Folio had been exciting for the Flood children as they had never been in a car before, let alone a minibus. They had travelled around on broomsticks and in Winchflat's Zoomy Thing,[15] both of which most people would think was far more exciting, and of course five of them went halfway round the world each day on a magic dragon bus to and from school. However, like most things that seem ordinary, the very first time you do them they're quite exciting.

---

[15] *See* The Floods 4: Survivor, The Floods 5: Prime Suspect *AND* The Floods Family Files *for more information about Winchflat's Zoomy Thing.*

Unlike the usual long, slow, boring drive to a holiday destination, this drive was a bit different. For one thing, they never had to stop for fuel. Whenever a hoon went racing by in a dangerous way, Mordonna clicked her fingers and the hoon's petrol simply vaporised from their tank and reappeared in the minibus tank. And, of course, as soon as they approached any traffic lights, the lights instantly changed to green.

'You know, that's quite amazing,' said Mr Hulbert, 'because lights usually turn red when I drive up to them.'

The hotel that Mordonna had booked was the best in town, five stars and staggeringly expensive. She figured, quite correctly, that if they went to a lesser quality hotel, they might be turned away. Obviously only seriously rich people stayed at the Hotel Splendide, and seriously rich people could be as weird and eccentric as they liked because they were seriously rich, and this meant the hotel staff were used to all sorts of strange visitors.

'After all,' said the manager to the concierge after the Floods had booked in, 'wiz ze sort of money zey are paying, zey can have three heads and be married to an 'ippopotamus if zey want to.'

'Or,' he added as Winchflat walked past with Queen Scratchrot on his back, 'zey can even live in a backpack. Alzough, of course, it must be a nice designer backpack like zat one, not somezing cheap and plastic from a street market.'

Mordonna had booked the whole of the top floor of the hotel for the two families. This meant that they would not be disturbed by other guests and everyone could have their own bedroom and

sitting room and ensuite bathroom.

The reception of the Hotel Splendide was indeed splendid. Huge crystal chandeliers hung down from an ornate ceiling that was decorated with gold leaf. Big soft velvet sofas and armchairs sank into a thick red carpet and rich, chinless old aristocrats sank into the armchairs, dreaming of the days long gone when they had had chins and working brains. Smooth waiters glided silently between the sofas bearing trays of china tea in china cups. As the doorman opened the shining brass doors and bowed his head, the Hulberts and the Floods felt as if they'd been transported a hundred years into the past. Even the three flies that had sneaked in with them buzzed very, very quietly.

'I think this is all a bit posh for us,' said Mr Hulbert in hushed tones. 'I mean, we're just simple people and this is terribly grand.'

'And I imagine it's, er, quite expensive,' said Mrs Hulbert.

The children, even baby Claude, stood in

complete silence with their mouths hanging open. For Satanella this was a good move as two of the three flies flew down her throat. Normally Merlinmary would have said it wasn't fair that her sister had got two flies to eat while she hadn't, but even she was overawed by the place and kept quiet.

'Absolutely,' said Mordonna. 'In fact it's very, very, very expensive – but don't worry, it's our treat.'

'But, but, but . . . we can't possibly let you pay for us,' said Mr Hulbert, who imagined his entire life savings being swallowed up just buying a sandwich.

'You're forgetting one thing, my dear Mr Hulbert,' said Mordonna. 'We are wizards, so we can get money out of thin air.'

And to prove it, she clicked her fingers and a gentle rain of one-hundred-dollar notes floated down from the ceiling until the entire floor was covered in them.

'Of course, if we had been in a cheaper hotel it would only have rained ten-dollar notes, and if

30

we had been in a really cheap bed and breakfast we would have been showered with coins, which can be very painful,' said Mordonna.

'So we insist on paying for everything,' she continued, swishing through the hundred-dollar notes to hand Mr and Mrs Hulbert each a glass of Krug Clos du Mesnil 1995 Champagne.[16] 'And that means everything. I want you to have the full beauty and spa treatment and every other luxury the hotel has to offer.'

'Well, I don't know about that,' said Mrs Hulbert, panicking at the thought of complete strangers seeing bits of her that even she hardly ever looked at. But after Mordonna said she insisted on it and that as they were on holiday it was all right to try new experiences, Mrs Hulbert began to feel quite excited by the prospect.

Mr Hulbert felt quite excited too, though he wasn't sure why, because excited wasn't something he had had much experience of.

---

[16] *One of the world's most expensive champagnes, costing around US$750 a bottle.*

'This is nice,' Mrs Hulbert said to her husband as champagne bubbles fizzed up her nose. 'It's a bit like your grandmother's dandelion cordial.'

'I wouldn't go that far, dear,' said Mr Hulbert, 'but it is rather good. What's this funny white stuff, Nerlin? It's a bit salty – reminds me of salt and vinegar chips.'

'It's Almas Caviar,'[17] said Nerlin. 'Not bad, is it?'

When they had all unpacked and freshened up, the two families went downstairs for lunch. As Mordonna had predicted, no one batted an eyelid.

'Though I wouldn't mind if they battered an eyelid,' said Morbid. 'They're delicious.'

'I'm afraid we'll have to make do with human

---

[17]   *US$25,000 a kilo. This is **NOT** a typing mistake!*

32

food,' said Mordonna. 'At least while we're in public. Of course, back up in our rooms it's a different matter.'

'Umm, yes, I've already had a bit of a problem with that,' said Merlinmary. 'My room's got a thing called a spa bath with all these jets of water and bubbles, and when I put my late night snacks in it to keep them fresh, it sucked all their legs off. Green Patagonian Newts without their legs are disgusting.'

'I'll see if I can make a Newt-Legs-Out-Of-Spa-Jets-Retrieval-Device,' said Winchflat. 'I brought my tools with me just in case. Then we could stick them back on with my Underwater-Newtral-Adhesive.'

'And just to be on the safe side, I've told the manager that we'd rather not have the maid go and tidy our rooms up every day,' said Mordonna. 'Humans can get very funny about amphibians and spiders.'

'Good idea, Mother,' said Valla. 'I hate to think what the maid would do if she saw the Giant

Leeches floating in *my* bath – not to mention the three sheep I've got in the wardrobe to feed them with.'

The Hulberts, who had been looking forward to lunch, had gone rather white while the Floods discussed their snacks, and decided to have salad instead of cutlets. Baby Hulbert, Claude, who had just begun to walk in that strange way that toddlers do,[18] was sitting under the dining table sharing a bone with Satanella. They both knew that anything green, unless it was meat with bacteria living on it, should be left growing in the ground and never put in your mouth or even on your dinner plate.

The waiter took it all in his stride when he asked the Floods how they would like their steaks and they said 'alive'.

'Just tell the chef to walk past the oven with them on a plate,' said Nerlin. 'In fact, it would be better if he ran past the oven . . . or perhaps you could just bring the cow in here and we'll help ourselves.'

---

[18] *Toddler walking involves looking at someone, setting off towards them and then walking in a completely different direction straight into a table because their brains haven't been properly connected to their legs.*

'And I'll have mine without the meat,' said Valla.

'I'm terrible sorry, sir,' said the waiter. 'I didn't realise sir was a vegetarian.'

If he hadn't already been whiter than a bleached skeleton, Valla would have paled at hearing the V word.

'Oh my goodness, no, no,' he said. 'I meant just bring me a cup of cow's blood.'

Mrs Hulbert turned as pale as Valla and was very relieved when Mordonna suggested that from now on the two families should probably eat at separate tables.

'Because we might need to sneak a few things in to spice up the food,' said Mordonna. 'I mean, humans might think chocolate pudding and ice-cream is wonderful, but us wizards need to add a few delicacies and flavour enhancers to make it edible.'

'I don't want to ask you what sort of delicacies,' said Mrs Hulbert, 'but I can't help myself.'

'Funny, isn't it?' said Mordonna. 'One thing that wizards and humans have in common is an

irresistible fascination with things that make you feel sick.'

'So what sort of things do you put in the ice-cream?' Ffiona asked.

'Well, my favourite is woodlice,' said Betty. 'You should try it, Ffiona. You've no idea how much better caramel sauce tastes when there are things wriggling in it.'

'Not to mention the excitement of trying to spear them before they run away,' Morbid added.

'Mind you,' said Satanella from under the table, 'I quite like potatoes with my pudding, but I suppose that's because I come from Potato Patches.'[19]

'Not sure about the "pota" bit,' said Merlinmary, 'but I like toes.'

Mr Hulbert tried to shut out the conversation by humming to himself, but when one of Betty's wriggly things escaped from her plate and crawled

---

[19] *Potato Patches is a famous place in Tristan da Cunha, which is where Satanella was born – see* The Floods 3: Home & Away.

up his sleeve, no amount of humming could help. He dropped his spoon in his jelly and custard and ran out of the dining room.

'He's probably got one of those tummy bugs I was reading about,' said Mordonna. 'The travel magazine said people often get them on holiday.'

'Tummy bugs?' said Betty. 'They sound tasty. I wonder where you buy them.'

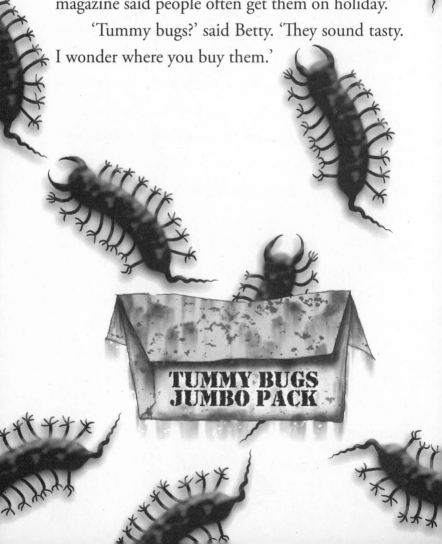

TUMMY BUGS
JUMBO PACK

After lunch everyone went down to the beach.

Like the town, it hadn't changed in a hundred years. There were rows of old-fashioned deckchairs full of people with bright pink sunburnt bodies all fast asleep with handkerchiefs over their faces.

'If they're all asleep,' said Betty, 'and if they've got their faces covered up, why don't they just stay at home in their back gardens?'

'I expect it's the change-is-as-good-as-a-rest thing,' said Nerlin. 'What I want to know is why all those people are in that angry water. Do you think we should go and help them?'

'No, Daddy,' said Betty. 'It's called the sea and it's not angry. That's called surf and what the people are doing is swimming.'

'Really? Why on earth would they do that? And what about those people with the doors?'

'Umm, what doors?' Betty looked out at the surf, confused.

'Look, those people in the water with the doors,' said Nerlin, pointing at one of them. 'They drag them out into the deep water and then try to stand on them. I mean, how stupid are they? If they want to stand on the doors they should just lie them down on the sand. Then they wouldn't keep falling off all the time.'

'I think it's called surfing,' said Betty. 'I had a look on Google before we left home.'

'Surfing?' said Winchflat. 'Well, I do that on the internet all the time. It's much better that way. I mean, you never fall off and you don't get wet.'

'Well, what's the point of it?' said Mordonna.

'I haven't the faintest idea,' said Betty.

'Didn't it say?'

'No. It's just another one of those mysteries of life that shows us how weird humans are,' said Betty, covering herself with one of the Witch Shrouds that Mordonna had brought with them to stop them getting horribly healthy-looking in the sunshine.[20]

'We're not weird,' said Ffiona.

'No, *you're* not, but most humans are,' said Betty.

'I'm afraid to say, you're absolutely right,' said

---

[20] *The shrouds were from the Collette Digintomb range of holiday wear, a consistent bestseller in Transylvania Waters's top department store Rabid Jones. Why it is so popular is a mystery as no one ever goes on holiday in Transylvania Waters.*

Mr Hulbert. 'Sometimes I feel quite depressed about being human.'

'If you ever want to change, you only have to say so,' said Mordonna. 'We could help you.'

She lay back in her deckchair, letting the sun melt her White Lead Blockout into every pore of her skin.[21]

'Could you make us into wizards?' said Ffiona. 'That would be so cool.'

'I'm afraid not,' Mordonna explained. 'Wizards and witches are unchangeable. We're the top species, which means no lesser species can become the same as us. Of course, in twenty-five billion and three years, when evolution has finished changing things, then the descendants of humans will probably have evolved into wizards.'

'Wow,' said Ffiona. 'You mean everything's evolving all the time?'

'Yes,' said Mordonna. 'In twenty-five billion

---

[21] *Another Collette Digintomb bestseller – filter factor 15,000, with added sulphuric acid for a whiter-than-white skin peel. See the back of the book for more information.*

and three years, the descendants of those jellyfish lying on the sand there will have become bank managers.'

'So if we did want to change,' said Ffiona cautiously, 'what could you change us into?'

'How about magpies?' said Mordonna. 'They're pretty clever, you know.'

'Or cockroaches,' Winchflat added. 'They're *really* clever.'

'I think we'll probably just stay human,' said Mrs Hulbert, looking faint.

'Yes, that's probably best,' said Mr Hulbert.

Winchflat had put Queen Scratchrot in her backpack down on the beach next to his chair and the Queen was enjoying herself playing with the sand. She scooped it up in her one remaining hand and let it run between her fingers, counting the grains as they drifted away.

'Six hundred and forty-three thousand, seven hundred and fourteen,' she said. 'When I was younger and had all my skin, I could hold over fifty million grains in the palm of my hand.'

'I thought you said you'd never been to the seaside before, Granny,' said Betty.

'I haven't, dear. It was back in the Transylvania Waters salt mines,' said the Queen. 'We used to go down and play there. It was a tradition for all royal children to be taken down there to throw stones at our enemies, who were kept in chains to dig out the salt. They were happy days. Well, not so much for our enemies, but we had a lovely time.'[22]

'What's that squeaking noise?' said Nerlin.

'Sorry, dear, it's me,' said the Queen. 'Got sand in my shoulder sockets.'

A gang of fifteen seagulls had landed on the beach and were now approaching the Queen. They were exceptionally big seagulls, and when they saw the Queen's bones poking out of the backpack they began to get very excited. They came rushing over and, before Winchflat could chase them away, one of them grabbed the Queen's left thigh bone and flew off.

---

[22] *This fine tradition is still carried on in many European countries to this day.*

'Oww, oww, oww, help,' cried the Queen as Nerlin chased the other seagulls away.

Mordonna threw a spell at the gulls and they all came crashing down on the sand.

'Listen, birds,' she said to them. 'One of you go after your mate and bring that bone back this very minute. That is the bone of a queen and when we put her back together again, we do not want to find any bits missing.'

The seagulls, who understood every word Mordonna said, all squawked in a loud, rebellious way, so Mordonna turned thirteen of them into Belgian taxi drivers.

'Right,' she said to the one remaining seagull. 'Off you go and get the bone. And don't think once you're out of sight I can't get you, because I can

46

and if you are not back here in ten minutes, I will turn you into a Belgian geography teacher who likes ballroom dancing and beige cardigans with horrible leather buttons.'

'Hello, good morning, and **where would you like to go to today?'**[23] said the thirteen Belgian taxi drivers to every single person they met as they walked up and down the beach.

---

[23] *When you see words written like* **This***, it means they are speaking Flemish. It also means that I am too poor to pay to get them translated into Flemish and my publisher is too mean to pay someone.*

47

Unfortunately there was not a single person on the beach who could understand them because they were all speaking in Flemish.[24]

'Go away,' was the reaction of most people, though two of them said, 'Can I have a vanilla ice-cream with chocolate sprinkles, please?'

The ex-seagulls could only understand Flemish so their usual reply was, '**Do you need a hand with your luggage?**'

After a while the taxi drivers all gathered in a group and began wandering about saying, '**I seem to have mislaid my taxi,**' in very distressed tones.

After eleven minutes, just as Mordonna was about to do her geography teacher spell, the two

---

[24] *A lot of Belgian people speak French and no Belgian people at all speak Belgian because there is no such language. You have to feel sorry for a country as big as Belgium that doesn't have a language named after it, but then neither do Switzerland, America, Canada, New Zealand nor, dare I say it, Australia. But at least our language doesn't sound like someone clearing their throat. I mean, if you had a cold and a blocked-up nose and someone said, 'How are you feeling today?', you might say, 'I'm feeling rather flemish.'*

seagulls returned and dropped the Queen's thigh bone at Winchflat's feet.

'Let that be a lesson to you,' said Mordonna after she had turned the others back into seagulls. 'Next time you're thinking about stealing a bone, make sure the creature it belongs to has finished with it. Now off you go and fly along the beach. Whoever drops the biggest mess on a sunbathing tummy will get this lovely big prawn.'

'This holiday stuff's fun, isn't it?' she said when the birds had flown off.

All along the beach there were angry cries as everyone got dive-bombed by the seagulls.

Winchflat, who had stayed behind in the hotel checking his email, now joined his family on the beach. He seemed to have collected a troupe of small boys, who were trailing behind him with their mouths open and pointing. This was because Winchflat was entirely encased in a massive ancient deep-sea diving suit with huge lead boots and a big brass helmet with a thick glass window. Winchflat stopped beside his parents and opened his window.

'I'm going for a swim,' he said. 'I may be some time.'

'Don't you need a boat with an air compressor and thick hoses to send air down to you?' said Mr Hulbert, who could remember seeing something similar in a book when he had been at school.

'Normally, yes,' said Winchflat, 'but I've made a few modifications. I will generate my own air internally.'

'Yeuww,' said Betty. 'That's gross.'

Winchflat closed his window and went down to the water's edge.[25] As he walked into the waves, the weight of his diving suit made him sink deeper and deeper into the sand. So by the time he had walked out about twenty metres, he was stuck fast and the only bit of him that wasn't buried was his head. And there he stayed as the waves crashed over him.

---

[25] *As Winchflat was in a really heavy suit with lead boots, I should have said that he 'stomped' down to the water's edge, but I vowed years ago that I would NEVER use the verb STOMP because it is the worst word in the world and is always used in really bad children's books. ALL books containing the word STOMP are bad (except this one).*

'I'm sure he knows what he's doing,' said Mordonna, who could not believe Winchflat could make a mistake.

None of them could. Since he had been a baby, Winchflat had been the family genius. He had only put a foot wrong once and that had been when he had been building his girlfriend Igorina and had put the left foot on the right leg. Even then he claimed he had done it for artistic reasons and not because he had made a mistake.

'With her feet on opposite legs,' he had claimed, 'if she ever tries to run away, she'll just keep ending up back here.'

'I guess the seagull standing on Winchflat's head is probably part of a brilliant experiment,' said Nerlin.

'It's probably something to do with sand,' said Merlinmary. 'He's probably studying the interactions between the grains in a sort of space–time continuum kind of way, taking into account the ectoplasmic gaps and interdependent relationship between the, umm, er . . .'

'What are you talking about?' said Betty.

'I haven't the faintest idea,' said Merlinmary, 'but I heard Winchflat say it once.'

'Well, I think he's stuck,' said Betty.

'Sweetheart, he's a wizard,' said Mordonna. 'Of course he's not stuck. All he has to do is click his fingers and say a spell and he can be out of there in a second.'

'No, he's stuck,' Betty insisted. 'And he's stuck so fast he can't even move his fingers to click them.'

'I suppose you could be right,' Mordonna admitted. 'We'll just leave him there a bit longer and see if he is or not.'

'How much longer?' said Betty as the tide came in a bit more and began to cover Winchflat's window. 'That man's just tied his boat up to that

ring on top of Winchflat's helmet and the whole thing will be completely under water soon.'

As the tide turned, Betty waded out into the water and tapped on the top of the helmet.

'Are you stuck?' she shouted.

Winchflat was stuck like toffee to a blanket, but he refused to admit it. He shook his head.

'See,' said Mordonna when Betty returned. 'I told you he wasn't stuck.'

'He's lying,' said Betty, 'but if that's how he wants it, fine. We'll just leave him there.'

And then everyone went to sleep for the rest of the afternoon.[26] Then they woke up and went back to the hotel for dinner which, because it was mostly human food and not wizard food, the Floods wished they had stayed asleep for. Except for the bit when Valla did a magic spell that made all of the wax in all the diners' ears fly across the dining room towards the dessert trolley and mix itself into the trifle.

---

[26] *Sleeping is a popular holiday pastime among humans because large bits of holidays are too boring to stay awake for.*

'This,' said Mr Hulbert to his wife, 'is the best trifle I have ever tasted, just like your mother's.'

Even Merlinmary's miniature sharks in everyone's coffee cups couldn't top the trifle trick.

Around two o'clock in the morning, a shoal of Blue Burrowing Stupid Fish[27] burrowed down past Winchflat's right hand, which gave him enough movement inside his diving suit to click his fingers and get himself free. By the time everyone woke up the next morning, he had got rid of the diving suit and pretended nothing had happened.

'Well, it's nice to know that he's human like the rest of us,' Nerlin said to Mordonna over breakfast, 'and not some super-genius.'

'The rest of us aren't human,' said Mordonna. 'We're witches and wizards.'

---

[27] *They are called Stupid Fish because if you are a fish that is meant to swim around, but you burrow two metres into the sand and then burrow out again, you are a very stupid fish.*

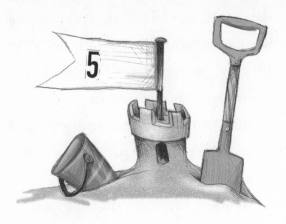

After breakfast, Betty and Ffiona raced back to the beach again. There was a big sign stuck into the sand. It said:

SANDCASTLE
BUILDING
COMPETITION
TODAY
FANTASTIC PRIZES

All along the beach there were groups of children digging holes and piling buckets of sand on top of each other. Most of the castles were pretty ordinary: a tower at each corner and a moat round the outside where younger brothers and sisters kept pouring water they'd brought in buckets from the sea. Of course, since sand is useless at holding water, no sooner had they tipped the water in than it soaked away. One or two children had tried to be clever and dug a canal down to the water's edge so that as each wave landed on the shore some of its water ran into the moat. This meant that those castles got washed away because the tide was coming in. The day was not only destined to end in tears, but start and continue in tears too.

'Look at them all,' said Betty as she and Ffiona walked along the beach. 'They're useless.'

'I bet we could do better,' said Ffiona.

'We could do much better than better,' said Betty, 'especially if we use a little bit of magic.'

'I thought your mum banned you from doing magic 'cause it always goes wrong.'

'Not always,' said Betty. 'Anyway, we'll only use a little bit of magic and we won't tell her. No one will know.'

'OK,' said Ffiona.

'We'll go up the far end of the beach,' said Betty. 'It's quieter along there. Can you run back and ask Winchflat if he'll give us a hand? We could do with a couple of his inventions.'

The one type of magic that Betty was very good at was housework, though of course housework is not so much magic as a terrible curse. Mordonna had made sure very early on that this was an area where Betty would always get it right so she would never have an excuse not to take the rubbish out or shampoo the rats.[28] So while Ffiona ran to get Winchflat, Betty flattened a large patch of sand

---

[28] *Of course, if you are a witch or wizard you quite often bring the rubbish in rather than take the rubbish out, especially if you live surrounded by humans like the Floods do. Winchflat had several cellars piled to the ceiling full of what he called 'really useful stuff', which you and I would call trash. In fact, 'going shopping' for Winchflat meant going to the local rubbish dump and collecting stuff.*

near the water's edge until it was as smooth as a fresh bedspread.

'Hey, stupid,' said a boy who was walking by. 'Are you going to build a castle there?'

'Yes,' said Betty, 'I am and it will be the biggest and best castle you have ever seen.'

'I don't think so, stupid,' said the boy. 'The tide will wash it all away before lunchtime.'

'The tide will not touch one grain of sand on my castle,' said Betty. 'It will flow into my moat, run round the castle walls and run away again. Which is what you should do.'

'I'm not afraid of you, stupid.'

Why is it that wherever you go in the world there is always a really dim-witted, spotty little boy who thinks he's really clever? Betty thought. She couldn't be bothered to argue with the boy. She just clicked her fingers and ten angry crabs ran out of the sea and clamped onto each of the boy's toes. This made the boy cry and fall on the ground, where one of the crabs decided it would be happier biting his nose rather than his little toe.

Mmm, needs ketchup

'MUUUMMMM!' the boy cried, but the wind was blowing in the opposite direction so his mother couldn't hear him.

'Now, now, little sister,' said Winchflat as he returned with Ffiona. 'Let the spotty boy go.'

Betty grumpily released the crabs, but Winchflat could see she wasn't quite finished.

'No, Betty,' he warned. 'There's no point in making him wet himself, he's got his swimmers on and they're wet already.'

Betty let the boy go, but she had her extra bit of revenge on him after all, watching his mother smack him for telling her that the pretty blonde girl with the big innocent eyes had made ten crabs bite him.

'Don't be so wicked,' his mother said. 'How can anyone make crabs bite you?'

'Did Ffiona tell you what we're going to do?' said Betty as the spotty boy threw himself on top of his little sister's sandcastle in a terrible tantrum.

'Yes, she did,' said Winchflat. 'So I popped back home in my Zoomy Thing and made a couple of things to help you.'

The first one looked just like the sort of bucket you would use for making sandcastles, except that each time you tipped the sand out, it instantly filled itself up again without you having to do it.

The second invention was something that was guaranteed to make Betty and Ffiona's castle one that would not only win the competition, but be remembered for many, many years to come.

Winchflat's iGlueatron could stick absolutely ANYTHING to ANYTHING else. You could stick water to the ceiling, jelly to a non-stick saucepan, and kittens to clouds. It could even stick brains inside a politician's head, but you had to put a lot of white ants in the politician's ear first to eat all the wood that was filling up the space where normal people kept their brains.

'Do you think we should wait until it's dark?' said Ffiona. 'I mean, we don't want to attract a crowd.'

'Well, it would be kind of cool for everyone to come down tomorrow morning and find it

here,' said Betty, 'but the competition finishes this afternoon, so if we want to win that, we've got to do it now.'

'I've got an idea,' said Winchflat, trying to restore his genius image after his swimming mistake. 'In fact, I've got thousands of ideas and they keep rushing round inside my head and crashing into each other and having baby ideas so I end up with more and more of them . . . but I do have two ideas to do with building your sandcastle.'

'What are they?' said Betty.

'Well, the first one is that we could all get inside my Zoomy Thing and go to the Sahara Desert to visit my old friend Lord Clacton. We could build the castle there and then bring it back here.'

'I'd rather not,' said Ffiona. 'That machine of yours makes me travel sick.'

'OK then,' said Winchflat. 'Plan B. You start building the castle and if people get inquisitive, I'll cover the sky with thunderclouds that'll make it as dark as night. If that doesn't keep them away, I'll make the clouds rain like the Niagara Falls.'

'Won't that wash our castle away?' said Ffiona.

'No, because it won't rain within the small circle where we are and also because my iGlueatron will make your castle totally one hundred per cent waterproof,' Winchflat explained. 'So even if the tide comes in and covers it, not one single grain of sand will move.'

'Wow,' said the two girls and started building.

At first their sandcastle looked like most of the others along the beach, with buckets of sand tipped out to make little towers and holes poked in them with little fingers to look like windows. But soon Betty and Ffiona got into the rhythm and began to progress beyond that, with the help of Winchflat's inventions. Their towers grew taller. The windows all looked like proper castle windows with round tops and fancy carving round the edges and, if you looked closely, there even seemed to be lights on in some of the windows.

As they added more and more, their sandcastle

became a scale model of Castle Twilight, the ancient home of the Kings of Transylvania Waters, where Mordonna had grown up.

This was amazing because neither Winchflat nor Betty had ever been there or even seen a picture of the place, but obviously the image of this incredible and unique building was buried in their genes. And Ffiona didn't even know there was such a place as Castle Twilight.

As the sandcastle reached shoulder height, a few people began to show interest and walk along the beach towards them. They were mostly the parents of children whose own castles were nowhere near as good. There was also a small brown dog who thought the castle looked like a tree and was overcome with an uncontrollable need to pee on it. When he did, there was a little flash of lightning and the dog ran off yelping in a cloud of scorched fur.

Seeing the crowd start to gather around them, Winchflat muttered under his breath and the sky grew as dark as night. Most people ran up the beach to take shelter, but a few still came nearer. Winchflat

muttered another spell and it began to rain, not a few drops building up into a storm but an instant torrential downpour like a burst water tank. It came down so heavily and so suddenly that everyone out in it was soaked to the skin in two seconds. It rained so hard that it got into the *Guinness Book of Records*. Other places it got included everyone's ears, which filled up and then overflowed down their necks. It was pointless trying to run for cover, though everyone did.[29] Everyone except Winchflat, Betty and Ffiona, who stayed perfectly dry in their little circle of sunshine.

'Won't all the other sandcastles get completely flattened?' said Ffiona.

'No, I thought about that,' said Winchflat. 'You're going to win anyway and it seemed really mean to wash all the others away, so I diverted the rain away from each one.'

It was true. Although the rain was so thick no

---

29 *It's weird, isn't it, but even when people are at the seaside in their swimmers and it starts raining, most of them run for shelter.*

one could see through it, directly above each castle was a little circle of clear sky.

As Betty and Ffiona added more and more turrets and castellations to their creation, it changed from being fantastic to being brilliant and finally it became a totally awesome masterpiece. The sea did, as Betty had predicted, flow in to fill the moat and, unlike everyone else's castle, the water stayed there. There were tiny baby sharks swimming round and round the castle, and a little drawbridge. And even though the tide was still rising, it didn't remove a single grain of sand from the enchanted model. The sand itself took on a magical quality, allowing the girls to mould and model it with incredible detail. They even changed the colour of the sand, so the roofs were grey like the lead of the original Castle Twilight.[30]

---

[30] *Castle Twilight's roofs had all been made of lead, but because lead is quite valuable, the King had sold it all and covered the roofs with grey painted cardboard which, of course, let in all the rain. And, as everyone knows, it rains almost every day in Transylvania Waters, so it was very, very wet inside the castle.*

The castle walls were not simply smoothed flat sand, but had all the lines where the stones joined together. If anyone had looked really closely, they would have seen that there was moss growing between the stones.

The finished sandcastle was a magnificent achievement. If it was a Rolls Royce, then all the other castles along the beach were bicycles with punctured tyres and rusty handlebars.

And yes, there really were lights on in some of the windows and mysterious moving shadows in some of the rooms, as if there were real miniature people inside. This effect was created by Winchflat, who had dressed a team of hermit crabs in tiny costumes and trained them to walk upright on their back claws, but you had to look really, really close to tell.

Winchflat took a tiny Transylvania Waters flag out of his pocket and stuck it in the roof of the tallest tower.

'There we are,' he said. 'Finished.'

He clicked his fingers and it stopped raining.

He clicked them again and the black clouds formed a long line and went off to rain on Belgium, which was a shame because stage two of that year's Tour de France cycling race was going through there that very day.

At five o'clock the judges walked along the beach looking at each of the thirty-two sandcastles. Thirty-one of them got equal second prize, which was a bucket and spade and a DVD called *How to Build Sandcastles*. Betty and Ffiona's castle won, in a judges' decision that was almost unanimous except that one judge had a son who had built one of the other castles, so he wouldn't vote for Betty

and Ffiona's castle even though it was clearly the best.[31]

The first prize was a family ticket to the local theatre to see the current seaside holiday show.

'Brilliant,' said Betty and Ffiona, neither of whom had been to the theatre before.

'Brilliant,' said Mordonna, Nerlin and everyone else when they showed them the ticket. No

---

[31] *There's a judge like that in every competition.*

one else in the family, apart from Queen Scratchrot, had ever been to the theatre either.

'I went to the theatre lots of times when I was young,' said the Queen.

'Really, I didn't know that,' said Mordonna.

'It was before you were born,' said the Queen. 'In fact, it was where I met your father.'

'What did you go to see, Granny?' said Merlinmary.

'Oh, I didn't go to see anything,' said the Queen. 'I was on the stage. I was one of the actors in a group of travelling players called the Mysterious Monarchs. All the actors were princes and princesses and we performed wonderful magical plays and exotic variety shows.'

'Wow, Granny, who would have thought?' said Betty.

'Well, not me,' said Mordonna. 'Why haven't you ever told us about it before?'

'Well, it all came to a rather tragic end,' said the Queen, 'and I'd rather not talk about it.'

'Oh go on,' said everyone, 'please.'

'No, it's too upsetting,' said the Queen.

'We'll polish your bones with linseed oil,' said Winchflat.

'And beeswax,' said Betty.

'With live bees?' said the Queen.

'Yes.'

'Oh, all right then,' said the Queen, arranging her loose bones as tidily as she could before pulling the zip in the top of the backpack tight around her neck.

She suspected that she might get quite emotional when she told them all her story and she wanted to make sure it was only her emotions that got carried away and not her ribs or any of those little tiny bones that are always so hard to find again.

'What none of you know,' she began, 'is that my husband, the mean, horrible, fat King Quatorze, was not my first true love. No, my first love,' and here she blushed as only a skeleton with virtually no skin left on it can blush, 'was the dashingly handsome, incredibly rich, but not very intelligent Prince Wynegum of Patagonia.'

'Patagonia? That's where we go to school, Granny,' said Merlinmary. 'I never knew there was a Patagonian royal family.'

'Prince Wynegum was the last,' said the Queen sadly. 'We were to be married and carry on the royal line so that Patagonia could once more claim its place as a leading world power.'

'So what happened?' said Mordonna.

'We were touring small country towns in Belgium,' the Queen continued. 'I said no, let's go to Wales or Tasmania, but I was overruled. I could sense impending doom. Have I ever told you that I have an unerring ability to sense impending doom?'

'Yes,' said everyone, beginning to sense impending boredom.

'Well, we were performing in the little town of Silly[32] on a cold December night. My beloved was about to do his high-wire act, where he walked blindfolded above the stage reciting Shakespeare's

[32] *Yes, there really, really is a place in Belgium called Silly.*

The Tempest and juggling seven pork pies and a Jell-O model of the Eiffel Tower, before leaping into a bowl of custard balanced on a small boy's head. This was nothing unusual. He had performed this act dozens of times, on several occasions with his trousers on fire, and even once with seven live chickens down his trousers – not at the same time his trousers were on fire, of course – but this night was different,' said the Queen.

She fell silent and for a few minutes no one said anything.

'Go on, Granny,' said Betty.

'Well, on this particular night there was a terrible storm in Silly. The thunder and lightning were so loud you could hardly hear yourself speak, even on stage. Prince Wynegum, being right up near the roof on his high wire, could hear nothing but the hail crashing on the roof. But, being a true professional, he didn't let that stop him. He began his walk and was halfway across when the biggest thunderclap ever recorded in the whole of Europe exploded above his head. The roof split open and a

massive bolt of lightning crashed through, looking for some metal. It found some – my beloved's crown. He lit up like a firework, and the audience, thinking it was part of the act, cheered their heads off as my darling flew up into the air and came down headfirst into the bowl of custard, cooked to a crisp. As the storm died down, the theatre was filled with the smell of burnt custard and roast prince. I have never been able to eat either since.'

'Oh my goodness,' said Mordonna.

'What happened to the boy who had the bowl of custard on his head?' said Morbid.

'We never saw him again,' said the Queen. 'Though there are stories that his ghost appears in the Silly theatre every time there is a thunder storm.'

'Does my father know this story?' Mordonna asked.

'Of course not, darling,' said the Queen. 'He is so stupid and so vain, he thinks it was his charm that won me over.'

'You're kidding,' said Mordonna.

Winchflat couldn't quite understand why, considering his grandmother was a powerful witch, she hadn't just cast a spell to make the King nicer.

'Some things are just too damaged for magic to fix,' said Queen Scratchrot, reading her grandson's mind. 'Believe me, I tried, but the best I could do was remove the ugly boils from his neck – and even that didn't work properly. They didn't so much go away as move down to his bottom. Still, it meant

I didn't have to look at them any more, because I can honestly say in all my years of marriage to the King, I never once saw his bottom.'

'Yeugh, Granny,' said Betty.

'Too much information,' said Mordonna with a shudder.

'So how did you actually meet him?' asked Winchflat.

'He was standing outside the stage door of the theatre one night asking every single person who came out if they would marry him. His parents had kicked him out of Transylvania Waters and told him he couldn't go back until he was married,' the Queen explained. 'Everyone else said no, of course, but when he asked me, I was so depressed over losing my sweetheart that I said, "Yeah, whatever," and before I knew it I was being whisked away in a coach and we were married before we reached the border.'

'How awful,' said Mordonna, who had married Nerlin for love and his incredible good looks.

Everyone felt rather depressed after the

Queen's sad story, but fortunately by then it was time to go back to the hotel for dinner.

It wasn't until they were all sitting down in the dining room that they realised one of the children was missing.

Satanella.

'Well, where is she?' said Mordonna when Betty said she couldn't find her. 'She was on the beach with us, wasn't she?'

'I don't know where she is,' said Betty when she came down from checking their rooms. 'I've looked everywhere.'

'She's probably playing with the baby Hulbert.'

'Claude,' said Betty.

'Yes, that one,' said Mordonna. 'You know how they adore each other.'

'No, she's not, that was the first place I checked. Claude's having his bath. He managed to get an incredible amount of sand in all his chubby creases, not to mention quite a lot of seaweed up his nose.'

'OK, so let's try to remember the last time we saw her,' said the Queen.

'It was on the beach,' said the twins. 'We were throwing sticks in the sea for her.'

'She didn't get washed away by that angry water, did she?' said Nerlin, looking quite alarmed.

'Or eaten by a shark?' said Merlinmary, imagining her sister all chewed up in little bits.

'There was a shark, but Satanella chased it and it swam off terrified,' said Morbid.

'Wait a minute,' said Valla. 'I saw her going off along the beach and that was after the stick throwing.'

They worked out that early that afternoon had been the last time any of them had seen Satanella.

'I bet she was going off after a scent trail,' said Betty. 'Satanella can't resist a good smell.'

The family agreed that Betty could be right. Like all dogs, Satanella was prone to picking up those scents that can hypnotise dogs so much that, no matter what else is going on around them, they are in a little world all of their own. You could

drop a bomb, make it rain lamb chops and throw a million red rubber balls, but nothing would be able to pull them away from the irresistible scent trail. The trail could go underground, up a tree, across a river, under a warthog's armpit and even into the finest Belgian sausage factory, but the dog would follow it to the ends of the earth.

'I hope she hasn't gone to the ends of the earth,' said the Queen. 'Little dogs do that, you know.'

'Well, we'd better go after her,' said Mordonna. 'Winchflat, I don't suppose you brought your Electronic-Hypnotic-Psychotic-Antibiotic-Smell-Tracker from home, did you?'

'Of course I did, Mother,' said Winchflat. 'I never go anywhere without it.'

'How can you be sure that it was a hypnotic, psychotic, antibiotic smell that Satanella was following?' said Betty. 'It might have just been a dead lobster.'

'I've thought of that,' said Winchflat. 'It has a Dead-Lobster-Antenna as well.'

'Should we take a collar and lead in case Satanella doesn't want to come back?' said Ffiona, who sometimes forgot that Satanella was Betty's sister and not just the family pet.

'A collar and lead?' said Morbid. 'You must be joking. The last person who tried to put a collar on our big sister is in traction and still undergoing finger transplants.'

'We could take Claude,' said Ffiona. 'If Satanella saw him, she'd come back straight away.'

'Darling,' said Mrs Hulbert, 'it's half-past Claude's bedtime and pitch black out there, and I've only just managed to get the last bit of seaweed out of his nose. You are not taking your baby brother back to the beach.'

'Don't worry,' said Winchflat, switching on his thermonuclear three-hundred-and-ninety-seven-LED torch. 'Betty and I will go and find her.'

Betty's hunch was right. Even without the help of Winchflat's Smell-Tracker, because they were wizards Betty and Winchflat were immediately able to detect that there was a powerful scent trail

running along the beach and off into the darkness. Because they weren't dogs like their sister, the scent did not entrance or hypnotise them.

'My equipment has analysed the smell as a very old baby's nappy wrapped around an even older crab's stomach,' said Winchflat. 'Pretty well irresistible to a dog, especially one with a nose as sensitive as Satanella's. Come on, we'll follow it.'

'How do you know she went that way?' said Betty. 'The trail goes in both directions.'

'My Electronic-Hypnotic-Psychotic-Anti-biotic-Smell-Tracker can tell that it came from that way and goes in that direction,' said Winchflat, pointing west. 'And I think Satanella would be much more likely to follow whatever is leaving the trail than to go back and see where it came from. I mean, she'd want to catch whatever it is that's making the smell, wouldn't she?'

'Yes, of course,' said Betty.

They followed the trail along the beach to the end of the bay. They climbed over some rocks and up to the top of the cliffs.

'Look,' said Betty as they squeezed under a wire fence, 'here's a bit of Satanella's fur caught on the wire.'

'Oh, that's good,' said Winchflat. 'If we can't find her, we'll just go home and clone another Satanella from one of her hairs.'

'That's not a very nice thing to say.'

'I think it was a joke,' said Winchflat.

'What do you mean, you *think* it was a joke?' said Betty. 'Either it was or it wasn't.'

'I think it was,' said Winchflat. 'I've been reading about jokes on the internet and I think that was one.'

'Well, it wasn't very funny,' said Betty.

'Are they meant to be?'

'Duh.'

'Oh,' said Winchflat. 'Obviously this whole joke thing is much more complicated that I realised. I think I'll stick to making subatomic nuclear fission anti-gravity shoes, though maybe I could make a Joke Detector with a little prod that could poke me when I'm supposed to laugh.'

'That would be a brilliant invention,' said Betty. 'There's billions of humans who could do

with one of them. It would make you really, really rich.'

The trail went all over the place in the soft grass on top of the cliffs, criss-crossing itself over and over again before going back down to the beach and heading back to where it had started.

'Are you sure your machine's working properly?' said Betty.

'Yes, absolutely.'

The trail ended about three metres from where they had started, but closer to the water's edge. It ended in a frenzy of footprints, some dog prints that weren't Satanella's and some human prints too.

'Looks like there was a fight or something,' said Betty.

'Well, there's no blood or fur,' said Winchflat.

'What's this?' said Betty, picking up a wallet.

'Ah,' said Winchflat after he'd looked through it. 'I think I know where our dear sister is.'

'Where?'

'This wallet belongs to the local dog catcher. I bet Satanella's locked up for being on the beach without a lead.'

'I'd like to know how on earth he caught her,' said Betty.

'Me too,' said Winchflat.

'Maybe he didn't,' said Betty. 'Maybe she ate him and all that's left is his wallet!'

'So why didn't she come back to the hotel?'

'If you'd just eaten a human being you'd be too full to climb up the steps from the beach,' said Betty. 'But actually, brother dear, the eating thing was a joke.'

'Oh. Well, in that case, I definitely need to make my Joke Detector.'

Betty and Winchflat went back to the hotel to tell their parents what they'd discovered. There was nothing that could be done that night, so first thing the next morning Mordonna and Nerlin went along to the council dog pound to rescue their daughter. Except when they got there, she didn't actually want to be rescued. She was tearing

round in a big cage playing with two Jack Russell terriers and an old football.

'You know you will be liable for a fine, letting your dog run around on the beach without a collar and lead?' said the dog catcher.

'I am pretending that I come from Belgium and I cannot understand a single word you are saying,' said Mordonna in perfect Flemish.

'Oh, from Belgium, are you?' said the dog catcher, disappearing into his office. 'Hold on. I'll get Maurice. He's one of your lot.'

'**Good afternoon, madam,**' said the dog catcher's apprentice.[33] '**My boss says that in order to get your dog back you will have to pay a fine for allowing it to walk on the beach without a lead.**'

'**Now listen, Maurice,**' said Mordonna, taking off her sunglasses and hypnotising the poor man, '**tell your boss that this dog is a Royal Belgian Spaniel and, as everyone knows, because they are royal they are allowed to roam free wherever and whenever they like. Furthermore, if I was to report your boss for locking up a Royal Belgian Spaniel, not only would *he* have to pay a huge fine, but you would both go to jail.**'

The apprentice told the dog catcher what Mordonna had said. The dog catcher had a very strong suspicion that there was no such dog as a

<hr>

[33] *Being an apprentice, he was only allowed to catch very old cats and very old ladies.*

Royal Belgian Spaniel, but his apprentice seemed completely convinced and he was Belgian, so the dog catcher decided they must be telling the truth and he opened the cage.

'I don't want to go,' said Satanella. 'I'm having a great time here with Ruby and Rosie.'

'Did that dog just speak?' said the dog catcher.

'Did that dog just speak?' the dog catcher's apprentice translated to Mordonna.

'Of course I did, you stupid man,' said Satanella, followed by, **'Of course I did, you stupid man.'**

The two men fainted.

Ruby and Rosie wanted to say, 'Did that dog just speak?', but dogs can't speak so they just looked as surprised as dogs can, which isn't a lot even if they feel it inside.

'Sweetheart, you know what happens to dogs who end up here, don't you?' said Mordonna.

'No, what happens?'

'Well, if no one comes to claim them and no

one wants to give them a new home, they keep them for a week and then they get . . . umm, err . . .'

'Sent to the big kennel in the sky,' suggested Nerlin.

'In that case, and seeing as how those two idiots are still unconscious, we'll just take Ruby and Rosie back to the hotel with us,' said Satanella.

'But maybe they have an owner who loves them and will come here looking for them,' said Mordonna.

'I'll ask them,' said Satanella, who could speak dog as well as human. She turned and conferred with the terriers for a moment. 'No, they were dumped on the beach by a really mean man who was jealous of them because his kids loved them more than they loved him.'

Mordonna picked up Ruby, or it could have been Rosie as they were identical,[34] and sniffed her fur. She closed her eyes and concentrated, then said, 'That'll teach people to be cruel to animals.'

---

[34]   *Apart from their names.*

'What have you done, Mother?' said Satanella.

'The mean man's wife and three children have just dumped *him* on a beach and driven off with his brother, who is really nice and was the man who the woman wanted to marry in the first place, except she got confused because she had lost her glasses,' said Mordonna. 'They will go to Canada and live happily ever after, having left a false trail that will send the nasty man to Belgium, where he will live miserably ever after like he deserves to.'

Normal parents would instantly say no to an idea like taking the two stray dogs home, but Mordonna and Nerlin were not normal parents. They were brilliant wizard parents, so they picked up the two little dogs and took them back to the hotel.

Normal hotels would instantly say no to anyone walking in carrying two dirty little dogs, but the Hotel Splendide was not a normal hotel. It was a super-luxurious, top-of-the-range hotel and the Floods had paid them a HUGE amount

of money to book the entire top floor for a week, plus the manager had seen Mordonna without her sunglasses on so was deeply in love with her. So when they did arrive back carrying Ruby and Rosie, he instantly sent a maid upstairs after them carrying two priceless bone china dog bowls containing the finest poached chicken.

It doesn't get any better than this, Ruby and Rosie thought.

(When a human sits back and says, 'It doesn't get any better than this,' there is always a tiny nagging voice in the back of their brains that whispers things like:

'Well, if this is as good as it gets, does that mean that from now on it's all downhill?'

or, 'Are you telling me that no one could be more perfect than your husband/wife?'

or, 'Oh, come on, surely you'd like a bigger house/ car/iPod than this?'

There was no nagging voice in Ruby's or Rosie's head. And there are no nagging voices inside the heads of wizards and witches, because when a wizard or witch sits back and says, 'It doesn't get any better than this,' they are always right. It isn't because they want less, but because they have the power of magic. Their husbands/wives really are perfect[35] and so is their house and everything else. And if they change their mind, as

---

[35] *In the entire history of everything, there have only been two wizard divorces and they involved identical twins and two very cross-eyed witches who, after it had all happened, were still not completely sure they hadn't remarried the same person.*

everyone does from time to time, all they have to do is
a quick spell and everything is perfect again.

Satanella explained to her brothers and sisters
what had happened. It was because of Ruby and
Rosie that she had been caught in the first place.
Not only had all three of them been completely
hypnotised by the crab-in-the-nappy trail, they had
all become instant best friends and were having too
much fun to notice the dog catcher creeping up
on them. By the time Satanella realised what was
happening they were locked up in the cage in the
back of his ute on their way back to the pound. Of
course, being a witch, Satanella could have escaped
at any time and had actually intended to, taking her
new friends with her, but as they were having such
fun playing with the old football in the cage at the
pound, before she could put her plan into action
her mother and father had arrived and 'rescued'
them.

Claude was over the moon to see Satanella
again, and when he was introduced to Ruby and
Rosie he was over three moons. On their part, Ruby

95

and Rosie found Claude's nappy to be a wonderful new world of excitement – not quite as incredible as the one on the beach, but a constant panorama of always changing smells – and so they fell in love with him instantly.

'Dog, dog, dog, dog, dog,' Claude said, showing that he could recognise what they were

but wasn't able to count properly. He also said, 'dog, dog, dog,' whenever he saw his mother, his father, his sister and anyone else, including furniture and horses and goldfish.

The four of them spent the rest of the day running in and out of everyone's rooms and eating bits of poached chicken and fluff.

The sign outside the theatre said:

**THE WONDERFUL WORLD OF
WIZARDS!
STARRING
THE PHENOMENAL, THE AMAZING, THE
INCREDIBLE, THE MIND-BOGGLING
THE GREAT KLUNKO!!!
AND
THE SENSATIONAL BRENDA
MAGIC THAT WILL DAZZLE YOU!
YOU WILL NOT BELIEVE YOUR EYES!**

'I don't believe my eyes,' said Mordonna. 'We're going to see a wizard, or at least a human pretending to be a wizard. This should be fun.'

'Maybe he's a real wizard,' said Betty.

'The Great Klunko?' said Mordonna. 'I don't think so, not with a name like that. No, he'll be a sad middle-aged loser called Terence.'

Betty and Ffiona's prize was seats right in the front row, the best place to see everything, and the very best place to be when the Great Klunko called for volunteers.

The Great Klunko, who actually was a sad middle-aged loser called Terence, had seen better days. At least it is to be hoped he had, because if he was now at the height of his powers, he should have given up and got a job making sandwiches. He swept onto the stage in a long black cloak, a tall black cardboard hat and threadbare trousers that were coming unravelled at the hems.

The Sensational Brenda was worse. She was quite a lot larger than someone wearing a sequinned bathing costume and red high heels should have

been, and it appeared she had put her lipstick on with her eyes closed or in a dark room during an earthquake or both.

'Good evening, everyone,' called the Great Klunko.

'Good evening,' said three small children somewhere at the back of the theatre.

'I CAN'T HEAR YOU!' roared the Great Klunko.

'Then wash your ears out!' shouted someone. There were roars of laughter from the audience.

The look of resigned desperation that had been on the Great Klunko's face when he had walked on stage was now joined by a look of pathetic sadness.

The Sensational Brenda twirled around in her glittering costume. Some bits of her twirled faster than other bits and it was at least a minute before all of her caught up with itself and faced the audience again.

'Ladies and gentleman,' said the Great Klunko, 'a big hand for my assistant, the Sensational Brenda!'

'Hey, Grandma,' shouted a voice in the darkness, 'the old folks' home called, your dinner's getting cold.'

Over the years the Great Klunko and the Sensational Brenda had undoubtedly heard every single insult they could possibly imagine and had tried to develop thick skins so they could ignore

them. But although they managed to hide it very well, Mordonna could see the two performers were upset inside. She realised that even the most rubbish actor or performer had a dream inside their head of hitting the big time and becoming really famous. As time passed and they got older, that dream faded, but it would never go away completely. The Great Klunko and the Sensational Brenda must have put their dreams in a cardboard box right at the back of the cupboard.

Even though they hadn't done a single trick yet, it was obvious that the magician and his assistant were not going to be very good. There would probably be a couple of card guessing tricks, a coin being made to appear out of thin air, maybe a white dove and some vanishing stuff.

Mordonna decided to help them. She would put the Great into the Great Klunko and create a night that everyone in the theatre would remember for the rest of their lives.

'Show us your knickers, Grandma,' shouted the voice from the audience.

'I bet they're all big and baggy,' shouted a second voice.

'And brown,' shouted a third.

And tonight, Mordonna said to herself, *you three will most definitely vanish.*

She turned to see where the three boys were sitting in the darkness at the back of the theatre and, clicking her fingers, made one of the spotlights on the stage turn round and shine right at them. This, of course, made them all go instantly very quiet.

'You seem very enthusiastic young men,' said the Great Klunko. 'Why don't the three of you come up on stage and help me?'

Normally, he only invited one person at a time onto the stage, but Mordonna had done a little magic as he spoke. The three louts came down the aisle and blundered up onto the stage. Once everyone in the audience could see them, they weren't quite so brave and stood in a line looking stupid and embarrassed.

'Don't be shy, young man,' said the Great Klunko. 'You're a little treasure chest.'

He waved his hand over the first teenager's head and produced a gold coin. 'You're a regular gold mine, aren't you?'

He produced three more coins out of thin air. He clicked his fingers behind the boy's head a fourth time. At the same time Mordonna clicked hers and seventy-five-thousand two-dollar coins rained down around the boy and buried him up to his neck.

'Wha . . . eh?' said the boy.

The three boys struggled out of the pile and began grabbing as many coins as they could. This was a bad move because Mordonna rewarded their greed by changing every coin they had put in their pockets into slimy, smelly and very dead rats, with just enough not-dead ones to give each boy a rather nasty bite.

The Great Klunko and the Sensational Brenda were speechless, but only for a split second until Mordonna clicked her fingers a second time and the rats vanished.

'Now,' said the magician, under Mordonna's

control, 'I will transport all three of you to a far-off place. Drum roll, please.'

'Yeah, as if,' sneered one of the boys, who were just too stupid to know when they were beaten.

'As if, as if, as if,' chanted the other two and then all three sang, 'Here we go, here we go, here we go.'

The Sensational Brenda opened the door of a black cabinet at the back of the stage. Everyone in the audience knew that the cabinet must be standing over a hidden trapdoor in the floor so that when the door was shut, whoever was inside would fall through the hole onto a big mattress underneath the stage.

The three young men all squeezed inside the cabinet. Brenda locked the door with five chains and ten padlocks and then the Great Klunko said the magic words.

'Alakazoo, alakazaam, alakaseltzer . . .'

What should have happened next is that Brenda should have pressed a hidden button, which would let off a big flash of magnesium smoke while

the trapdoor opened and the three louts fell through
on to the mattress.

But what actually happened was far more exciting.

The cabinet rose in the air until it was three metres, four metres, five metres above the stage. The whole theatre held its breath as it hung in the air surrounded by tiny sparks of lightning.

The lightning grew stronger, big flashes sparking all around the cabinet and out over the audience's heads. For a whole minute the cabinet hung there defying gravity, and then there was an almighty clap of thunder and it came crashing down onto the stage, shattering into a thousand pieces. There was another blinding flash of light and there was the cabinet, all back in one piece, looking as shiny as the day it had been made. Its door flew open to reveal a few remaining flashes of lightning dancing around inside it and three pairs of shoes. The louts were nowhere to be seen.

The audience erupted in the loudest cheers the Great Klunko and the Sensational Brenda had ever heard in their whole forty-two years on the stage. In fact, if you added all the cheers they had

ever heard together, this was better.

'Quick, slip downstairs and see that the boys are all right,' the magician whispered to Brenda.

'But, but . . . I didn't press the button,' Brenda whispered back. She went to check the mattress below the stage anyway.

The audience were on their feet cheering for a full five minutes.

'They're not there,' said Brenda. 'There's no sign of them.'

Mordonna walked down to the edge of the stage, took off her sunglasses, looked up and caught the Great Klunko's eye.

'Don't worry,' she said. 'Just carry on with your act.'

The magician and his assistant both looked down at Mordonna and felt great waves of peace and happiness sweep over them. The happiness tide had been out for a very long time in their lives, so long that they had never expected it to return, but now they felt as happy as they had the day they had first met and fallen in love.

'Everything will be wonderful,' Mordonna whispered to them. 'Just do all your regular tricks and they will be brilliant.' She sat down again.

Meanwhile, in a sausage factory in a small town in Belgium – a factory that, many years before, had been a small theatre – three speechless louts had appeared in the Sausage Twisting and Snipping Room. Four young Belgian girls, who had been twisting and snipping sausages before sending them down the conveyor belt into the Sausage Boiling and Wrapping Room, stood open-mouthed as an ever-growing mountain of untwisted and unsnipped sausages began to pile up round their feet.

'Why is there a sausage factory underneath the theatre?' said one of the young men.

The four girls, who only spoke Flemish and knew exactly how to tell a local taxi driver where they would like to go, **screamed** and ran out of the room.

'I don't think we're underneath the theatre,' said another one of the young men.

They followed the girls out of the room, ran down a corridor and found themselves outside in the main street of Silly.[36]

'This ain't Port Folio, is it?' said the first lout.

'No, and it's not eight o'clock in the evening, either,' said the second, looking out the window at a sunny sky.

'I want my mum,' cried the third.

---

[36] *As I've said already, there really is a place called Silly in Belgium, but I don't know whether it really has a theatre or a sausage factory. So if you go there and can't find either, don't blame me.*

How the three of them got home again from a country where they couldn't understand a single word anyone said to them and where they had no money or shoes or passports or any signal on their mobiles is another story.[37]

Back in the theatre, the Great Klunko and the Sensational Brenda were going from strength to strength. Never in their entire career had they had such a wonderful and appreciative audience. And never in their entire career had all their tricks not only gone exactly how they were supposed to but ten times better.

Now the Great Klunko could not only guess which card the volunteer from the audience had picked, but he could make it vanish and reappear in the underpants of the person they had been sitting next to in the audience. And on top of that – and this was not something Mordonna had had any control over – the person with the card in their undies was a top television executive who happened

[37] *And much too boring to put in this or any other book. I mean, like, who cares? They're dumb louts and they deserved it.*

to be visiting his grandmother in Port Folio and had, against his wishes, been taken by the old lady to see the Great Klunko.

'Do I really have to?' he'd said, but now he couldn't believe his eyes.

Here in this little sleepy seaside town, where even the fish and chips had cobwebs on them,[38] was the greatest magician he had ever seen in his life, a man whose tricks seemed almost mystical. He would sign him up. He would call him The Man Who Put the Magic in Magician, and they would both become seriously famous and very seriously rich. The Sensational Brenda was probably not as young nor as beautiful as today's television audiences demanded, but the producer had never seen anyone, young, old, plain or gorgeous, who could juggle six eggs, throw them up into the air in a puff of smoke and have them come down as six live chickens. For an encore the Sensational Brenda then juggled six paper bags full of mushrooms that

---

[38] *One of the things that the Floods had discovered they really liked about Port Folio.*

changed into six pink pigeons that landed on the stage and turned into six cute puppies that could bark all the Beatles songs in perfect harmony.

At the end of the show the audience cheered so loudly that the Great Klunko and the Sensational Brenda had to come back for seven encores and then use some ear drops to stop their ears ringing. They only managed to make everyone go home when they both got inside the cabinet and made themselves disappear. They did not reappear in Silly, but back in their dressing room, where Mordonna was waiting for them.

'From now on,' she said, 'all your magic will be as brilliant as it was tonight.'

'We don't know how to thank you,' said the Great Klunko.

'Just do lots of brilliant magic for everyone,' said Mordonna.

'What happened to those three horrible boys?' said the Sensational Brenda.

'Who cares?' said Mordonna. 'And if you get any more troublemakers in the audience, just

put them in the cabinet. Nice people will just get transported to the theatre foyer, but troublemakers will end up on the other side of the world.'

As she left, the television producer arrived with a big fat contract and the three of them lived happily ever after in the Lap of Luxury, which is a very expensive seaside village in California with a tall fence all round it.

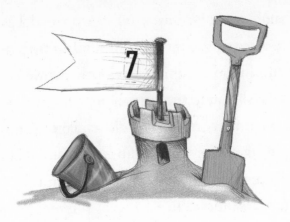

After almost a week, Betty and Ffiona's sandcastle still stood at the end of the beach as perfect as the day they had built it. The council had erected a fence round it with Keep Out signs, and a team of scientists were poking and prodding at the turrets with a whole barrage of high-tech equipment. Their instruments recorded nothing at all. Even the Sandometer, which should have told them the castle was made of sand, just showed a blank screen.

Most scientists think they are Very Important People with Tunnel Vision, which means that

although they tell everyone they are developing and discovering new and exciting things, they are actually just developing new and exciting names for things that everyone already knows about.[39] The scientists on the beach at Port Folio were exactly like that. It never occurred to them that magic might have something to do with the castle, because scientists don't believe in magic. As far as they were concerned, every single thing in every single place had a proper scientific explanation. If it didn't, then it obviously didn't exist – even if, like the wonderful sandcastle, they could see it with their own eyes.

When their twenty-five different bits of equipment showed them blank screens, they assumed that all twenty-five were faulty.

'They must have been dropped or got wet on their way here,' said the chief scientist, who then ordered all twenty-five to be replaced.

'These ones must have been dropped or got

---

[39] *Unless they are Wizard Scientists, who really do create and discover new and exciting things.*

117

wet too,' he said when the second lot showed blank screens.

Winchflat went along to the sandcastle every day and watched the scientists.

'Excuse me,' he called over the barrier. 'I think I can help you.'

'Move along, sonny,' said one of the Port Folio policemen, who were now on a twenty-four-hour guard around the sandcastle.

'But I can explain it all,' Winchflat insisted.

'If you don't go away right now, sonny,' said the second policeman, 'I'll have to arrest you.'

'Really?'

'Yes,' said the third policeman.

'I don't think that would be a very good idea,' said Winchflat and clicked his fingers.

Immediately all the seagulls on the beach gathered in a huge flock and dive-bombed the three policemen with such accuracy and attention to detail that in less than five minutes every square centimetre of their uniforms had changed from Official Policeman Blue to Unofficial Seagull

Guano White With Black Streaks.

'See, told you so,' said Winchflat. He clicked his fingers again, which made the seagulls call for reinforcements before they all dive-bombed the four scientists.

'We're going to the funfair,' said Betty when the family arrived at the sandcastle to check on the scientists' progress. 'Are you coming, Winchflat?'

'No thanks,' said Winchflat. 'I'm having too much fun here.'

'There's a circus too,' said Satanella. 'With performing animals.'

'I might come along later,' said Winchflat as his team of precision seagulls swooped down to give the policemen and scientists another coat.

Witches and wizards shouldn't really be allowed to go to funfairs because they turn them into unfairs. No matter how much the sideshow owners cheat, and they all do, wizards can always win the big prize on the top shelf that no one is ever supposed to get. If the last coconut you need to knock down is glued in to the shy, wizards just unglue it. If the

mechanical arm starts to move towards the five-cent whistle, wizards just concentrate and make it pick up the really good wristwatch. Of course the sideshow owners don't realise this is being done by magic because, like scientists, and most humans, they don't believe there is such a thing as magic.

Betty's favourite thing at funfairs was the big dipper. The bigger and dippier the better, but even the wildest ride in the world could always be made better with a bit of magical help.

'I think I might be very sick if I went on that,' said Ffiona, looking up at the huge wheel towering almost fifty metres into the sky.

'No you won't,' said Betty. 'You'll love it.'

And just to make sure nothing went wrong, she got her mother to do the I-Will-Not-Puke-Ever-At-All-Spell on Ffiona, and the Flying-Through-The-Air-Incredibly-Fast-Is-Brilliant-And-I-Love-It-More-Than-Anything spell too.

The two girls waited until they could get the front seat in the first car. Normally the roller-coaster went round the track once, which took about five

and a half minutes. With a snap of the fingers from Betty, this time it went round a lot quicker. Instead of slowing down as it reached the end, it kept speeding up until it was going so fast it kept leaving the track. By the time it came round for the third time it was travelling at over two hundred kilometres an hour and still accelerating. Apart from Betty and Ffiona, all the passengers were screaming at the tops of their voices. By the time it went round for the fifth lap all the people on the ground below were screaming too and running for the exits.

In one last brilliant circuit it left the track completely and soared up into the sky. It looped the loop over seven clouds, stood on its end, waited a second and then came screaming back towards the fairground so fast that it broke the sound barrier.

It shot round the track once more and then came to a nice slow stop at the finishing line.

Mordonna hadn't thought to do the I-Will-Not-Puke-Ever-At-All-Spell on Mrs Hulbert, which was a pity, because when she had seen her

daughter vanishing into the clouds as the roller-coaster went higher and higher, she went extremely white and threw up into her handbag.

'Wow, that was totally brilliant,' said Ffiona as she and Betty staggered around trying to get their balance back.

'Yeah,' said Betty. 'Now let's go and trash some boys on the dodgems before the circus starts.'

Even Ffiona could have trashed the boys, because when boys get into small cars they usually become very stupid.[40] So it wasn't really necessary for Betty to make massively thick sticky cobwebs full of horrible, biting, but not fatal, spiders fall down on each dodgem car until all seventeen cars with spotty young macho idiot boys driving them were completely jammed together like fish in a net.

'Have you ever set fire to a cobweb?' said Betty as she pulled up alongside the tangled mess.

'No,' said Ffiona. 'What happens?'

---

[40] *This can go on until about the age of fifty.*

'This,' said Betty and struck a match.

Of course she didn't really set the cobwebs on fire. She just held the flame close enough to make every single boy wet himself.

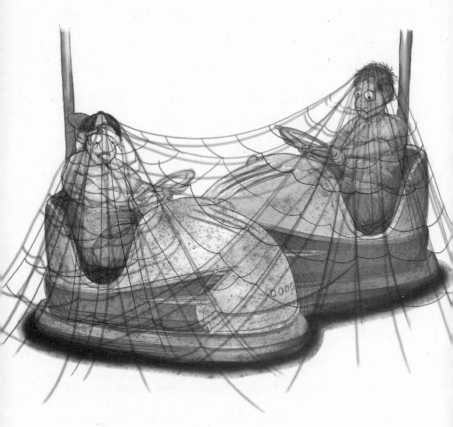

'Come on,' she said to Ffiona, 'the circus is about to start.'

124

The circus was one of those old-fashioned ones where wild animals are forced to do demeaning tricks, such as opening their mouths while their trainers put their heads in them or walking around on their hind legs dressed in human clothes.

Naturally, wizard circuses do not do this sort of thing. Wizard circuses have wizards doing incredible things, which the audience can do because they are all wizards too, but which everyone still enjoys seeing. Wizard clowns don't have red noses, big shoes and funny clothes. They all dress up like bank managers and lend each other money or else stick each other into filing cabinets. Wizard circuses do have some performing animals, but they fall into one of two categories. The first category is sheep and chickens, who are too stupid to realise they are being exploited, but are clever enough to realise that performing in a circus is probably better than getting roasted in an oven and covered in gravy. The other category is performing humans, who are also too stupid to realise they are being exploited, which is

why TV shows like *Big Brother* and *Idol* are so successful.[41]

The circus at the Port Folio funfair was not a wizard circus. It was the worst sort, full of depressed animals, and the Floods decided they would have to do something about it.

'Are you going to get the lion to close its mouth when the trainer puts his head inside it?' said Ffiona, when Betty told her their plans.

'No, tempting as it is, biting human heads off would probably be going a bit too far. Yes, it would be very entertaining with all that blood and guts, but the audience are mostly human and humans are a bit squeamish. I don't think they'd enjoy it very much,' said Betty. 'What usually happens in this sort of situation is that Mum casts a few spells to reverse everyone's roles.'

First of all some clowns came on and drove

---

[41] *That and the fact that the human audience are equally stupid. Actually, some of them are even more stupid, because they are the ones who were rejected from being on* Big Brother *or* Idol.

round the circus ring in their silly car with wheels that fell off. Then they threw water at each other and tripped over each other's great big clown shoes, usually landing face-down in custard pies. No animals were hurt or insulted during this bit.

But then the ringmaster stood in the centre of the ring and cracked a big whip as six beautiful white horses ran round and round, each one with a small poodle on its back.

Now, as anyone who owns a labrador knows, some animals actually like doing stupid things to make their humans happy. So before she did any circus magic, Mordonna looked inside each performing animal's head to see if they were happy or sad. Then she made her adjustments.

'They all hate the whip,' Mordonna whispered, 'and the ringmaster's wife doesn't give them enough to eat. Those poodles are quite a bit more intelligent than she is, too.'

So as the ringmaster flicked his whip back for another big crack, the three-metre braided leather thong wrapped itself round his body and

slapped him across the face. At the same time the six poodles stood on their hind legs and clapped with their front paws.

What happened next:

The horses raced out of the ring, galloped across the paddock, through the gate and away into the vast forest behind the town, where they still live to this day, eating soft green grass and leaves, drinking crystal clear water from mountain streams, raising a new generation of beautiful wild foals and generally thinking to themselves, Life does not get any better than this.

As the horses had run away through the town, the poodles had leapt off their backs and all six of them had ended up living with a little old lady who fed them lightly poached chicken and cuddled them in a big soft armchair in front of a big log fire.

Like the horses, the poodles and the little old lady all thought, Life does not get any better than this.

And of course they were right.

The ringmaster had a nasty red weal across his face from his whip that never quite faded. Circus ringmasters are quite often incredibly vain and pompous people who even go to bed in their top hats. This one was like that and, after Mordonna had given him exactly what he deserved for cracking a big whip at defenceless animals for twenty-seven years, he left the circus and moved away as far as he could from everyone to a remote run-down property where he spent the rest of his life growing rhubarb that was so sour no amount of sugar could improve it. His wife, who was just as vain, decided she could not love a man with a red scar on his face because it would clash with her new lipstick, so she ran away with the rhubarb inspector from a large supermarket chain and lived miserably ever after.

It rained a lot on the rhubarb farm and the ringmaster sat on his verandah staring out at his fields of mud and rhubarb and thought, It can't get any worse than this. Then the verandah collapsed on his head and he realised it could.

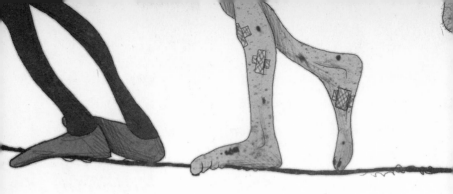

The next act was some acrobats. There were no animals in the act, but the acrobats were not very good. The only highlight was when one of them fell off, and even that wasn't so great because there was a safety net, so the only thing that got broken was a fingernail.

But then three of the clowns came back and this time they had five chimpanzees with them. The apes were dressed in copies of what the clowns were wearing – baggy trousers with big red spots and orange braces and silly bow ties.

Mordonna concentrated.

'The chimpanzees are really angry,' she whispered. 'They were all taken away from their families when they were babies and have never seen them since. This will take a bit of sorting out.'

'Will it be difficult to find their parents?' said Betty.

'No, that bit's easy,' said Mordonna. 'I can do a quick DNA test, transport it to a laboratory in the Congo and get them to do comparison tests on the International Chimpanzee DNA Database. We can do that before the first custard pie falls inside the first pair of clown trousers.'

'So what's the problem?'

'None of them want to go back to the Congo,' said Mordonna. 'They want to stay here and get revenge and they want to get it over and over again.'

She clicked her fingers and the oldest chimp came over and climbed

into her lap. As chimp and witch communicated telepathically, one of the clowns came marching over with a very angry look on his face.

'What do you think you are doing?' he snapped and, under his breath, he added, 'Just you wait until later, you little troublemaker.'

As he reached out for the chimp it screamed at him and bit him on the hand. The clown jumped backwards, tripped over his big silly clown shoes and fell flat on his back. Two other chimps raced over and threw custard pies at the fallen clown. Then the first chimp wiped them all over the clown's face . . .

. . . with her bottom.

The audience exploded with laughter. They all thought it was part of the show. As the two other clowns ran over, Mordonna clicked her fingers again and their trousers fell down, making them fall flat on their faces. The five chimpanzees ran round the circus ring grabbing all the ice-creams off the audience and throwing them at the three clowns. When the children saw what the chimps

wanted them for, they were only too happy to hand them over.

Now, what most people don't realise is that chimpanzees can actually talk and are a lot more intelligent than many human beings. They just pretend they can only grunt and aren't very bright to avoid the millions of problems that speaking with mankind would bring them. So while Mordonna was tempted to get the leading chimp to speak, she didn't. She sent her thoughts out into the fairground and searched through all the people working there until she found one with a kind heart. There were quite a few people with kind hearts, but Mordonna needed just the right one. She found the perfect person: Carla Divine, a girl of eighteen who wanted to be a clown, but wasn't allowed to because she was a girl.

While the five chimpanzees kept the three human clowns pinned to the floor with biting, bottom wiping and screaming, Mordonna cast her spell. Carla Divine left the coconut shy where she was working and went back to her caravan.

133

She locked the door and put on the secret clown costume she had made herself, but never told a single soul about. Whenever she put on the big, baggy red silk trousers and the huge spotty bow tie and the funny shoes, she was overcome with a feeling of extreme happiness. Once she had completed the picture by putting on the makeup with the big red clown grin, a little voice inside her head kept saying, *It doesn't get any better than this*, over and over again.

Then she marched into the circus tent and into the middle of the ring. Instantly the five chimps rushed up to her and kissed her hands. The chimps adored her because she had always treated them as her equals and preferred to be with them than most of the humans in the circus. This was because chimps, like labradors, spend huge amounts of time thinking, *It doesn't get any better than this*.[42]

The audience cheered and cheered.

Carla drank in the applause for a few minutes

---

[42]   *Even Belgian labradors think this.*

and then held up her hand. You could have heard a pin drop.

'Well, boys and girls,' said Carla Divine. 'What do we have here?'

The chimps jumped up and down and pointed at the three sticky, sawdust-covered clowns, who kept trying to stand up only to fall flat on their faces again. If it looked like one of them might manage to get to his feet, one of the chimps would bite him on the ankle.

'We have three very dirty clowns, haven't we, boys and girls,' Carla continued. 'And what do we do with someone when they get dirty?'

'BATH! WASH!' shouted eighty-seven hyperactive children.

'Yes, that's right,' said Carla, 'and with *lots* of water.'

Three of the chimps ran out of the ring. They ran back a minute later, each dragging a big hose.

'WASH, WASH, WASH, WASH!' chanted the audience in time to Carla waving her arms up and down.

While the clowns were being hosed down, the little girl sitting in the row in front of the Floods turned to her father. 'That was, like, the best circus I have *ever* been to,' she said. 'The chimpanzees were brilliant.'

What happened next:

The man who owned the circus knew a good thing when he saw it and Carla Divine was promoted from polishing coconuts to being chief clown. She was given a brand new caravan with enough room for her and the five chimpanzees to live in and, as the six of them sat around her stove toasting marshmallows, they all thought, Life does not get any better than this, *together.*

And of course they were right.

The three mean clowns were allowed to stay on as Carla Divine's assistants. You might think that they would never agree to that, but Mordonna cast a spell over them so they all thought that Carla Divine was a genius and the highlight of their week became giving the chimps a bubble bath on Friday nights.

Of course, the Floods didn't interfere with the acrobats or high-wire act.

'If humans want to risk serious injury to *themselves*, that's up to them,' said Mordonna. 'Though I think we need to get rid of the bouncing kittens. I'm sure they can't enjoy being dropped onto a trampoline from twenty metres in the air.'

'No,' said Betty, 'but they do look funny going up and down waving their little legs around, don't they?'

'Now, darling, that's not very nice, is it?' said Mordonna, doing her best not to laugh.

'Sorry,' said Betty.

'She's right, though, Mum,' said Morbid. 'They look hilarious.'

'Yes,' said Satanella, 'and besides, cats are evil little creatures. They're always trying to scratch me when I chase them.'

All of this was true, but it was cruel, and so Mordonna changed them into chickens.

'Which is probably just as cruel,' said Nerlin, 'but even funnier than the kittens.'

'Sorry,' said Mordonna. 'I am a witch. I am supposed to be a bit evil – and anyway, the one thing chickens spend every minute thinking about is being able to fly, and now they can. Sort of.'

After the horse and poodle and clown fiascos, the circus owner almost cancelled the highlight of his show, the lions.

'The way things are going tonight,' he said, 'it could end in serious injury to someone.'

But, like most so-called 'lion tamers', the Port Folio Circus's lion tamer was a short little macho loser who would never admit to being afraid of anything.

That was his first mistake.

As the lion tamer paraded around the ring, pushing out his chest and cracking his whip, the huge steel fence was locked into place and the three lions were pushed down the tunnel into the spotlight.

The lion tamer cracked his whip and the lions roared. Most people think that circus lions roar because they have been trained to, but they

actually roar because they are miserable and angry. It's only the whip and the tranquilisers that have been slipped into their water bowls that stop them acting like lions are supposed to.

I hate it when they're wearing socks. All the wool gets stuck in your teeth.

When the three lions were all sitting on their round boxes, the lion tamer stood in the middle of the ring and lifted his right arm above his head to give his whip a great crack to prove how macho he was. Just before the whip came down again, Mordonna clicked her fingers and the braided leather thongs turned into braided antelope's intestines[43] dripping with blood and smelling very, very delicious.[44]

It was hard to tell who moved the quickest, the three lions or the lion tamer. It was all a blur as they fled down the tunnel. Actually, it was only the lion tamer who fled. The lions chased.

What happened next:

Actually, what happened next cannot be written down for the following reasons:

---

[43] *No antelopes were harmed during the casting of this spell. Mordonna made them out of bits of old rabbits that had all died peacefully in their sleep.*

[44] *If you are a lion, that is.*

- *My publisher wouldn't let me as this is a children's book.*
- *You can guess anyway.*
- *Any really nasty, vicious stuff might not be too good for Mordonna's image.*

But everyone lived happily ever after, sort of. The lions were taken to a lovely huge wildlife park, which was better than going back to the wild because they didn't have to go and hunt for their dinner.

They spent their afternoons lying in the shade of a big tree thinking, Life does not get any better than this.

They also thought, I never realised that lion tamer could give you such indigestion.

The final act of the circus, which would have included the horses and poodles and lions, was a bit of an anti-climax.

What normally happened was that pigeons were released and flew around the big top in a terrified flock, crashing into the ropes and poles

before taking refuge on a perch right in the very top of the tent. Mordonna knew that there was only one way to get them down from there. After everyone had left, the circus owner would open the tap on a big cylinder of sleeping gas. The gas would drift up to the top of the tent and make all the pigeons pass out. One by one they would fall off the perch and fall down into the safety net, from where they would be stuffed back into their cages until the next performance. Needless to say, all that gas every day, and twice on Saturdays, made the poor birds feel horribly sick nearly all the time, so there was no way that Mordonna was going to let that happen ever again.

When Mordonna made a hole appear in the canvas, the pigeons couldn't believe their luck and flew off to join the horses in the forest.[45]

-----

[45] *Except for one even-dumber-than-normal pigeon, which flew straight through an open window into a kitchen. This was OK, because the kitchen belonged to a family who were so poor they normally only had porridge to eat and pigeon pie was something they had only ever dreamed of.*

'Great show,' said Betty as they walked back
to the hotel.

'Yeah, cool,' said Ffiona.

'Certainly not what I expected,'
said Mrs Hulbert.

Although Valla loved his family, he was by nature a solitary being. He imagined that one day he would meet the right girl and fall in love and get married. He realised that as the eldest of the Flood children it was his responsibility to carry on the great name of Flood, but for the moment he was happiest with his own company and the company of mysterious creatures of the night, who were dark and exciting to be with, but not the sort of beings you would marry or even take home to meet Mum and Dad.

So a holiday, to Valla, meant going out after

dark and wandering the lanes and alleyways and graveyards of the town. While most of Port Folio was asleep, he made new and exciting friends, many of whom lived under stones or in the dark recesses of family vaults. The undead, the freshly dead and the we-want-to-be-dead-but-cannot-die-because-of-an-evil-curse were the creatures Valla felt at home with. Most of them had long since lost their blood, which meant that Valla was never tempted to sink his teeth into their necks. It never ceased to amaze him that a lot of people didn't actually enjoy it when he did that.

Although it was a very small town, Port Folio had two undertakers. This was because it was the sort of place lots of old people went to live when they retired, and old people have a tendency to die more than young people, so there was always enough work to keep both undertakers busy. In fact, sometimes there was too much work and the richer families sent their dead relatives off by parcel post to the extremely expensive Di Calma Crematorium, where they sent the ashes back to

you in an exquisite urn cast from the finest bone china made with your relative's own bones.

Valla hated crematoriums. He thought turning dead bodies into little piles of ash was an unforgivable waste of so many useful things.

'It's not just the blood,' he said. 'I mean, look at my shoelaces. They're made from the finest human leg sinews, and my drink bottle is a famous athlete's bladder. There's just so much useful stuff in a dead body.'

'Absolutely, darling,' Mordonna agreed. 'Especially nowadays when we are all being told to recycle as much as possible.'

'And look at that lovely outdoor table and chairs that Father made from those old skeletons,' Valla continued.

'And if we didn't have those gorgeous skull-top bowls,' said Mordonna, 'what on earth would I use to make crème brûlée in?'

'I know,' said Valla, putting his favourite bookmark back in his journal, a bookmark that had once been someone's left ear.

As midnight struck, Valla took his cloak, wrapped it round himself and went out into the town.

'Don't eat anything I wouldn't, darling,' Mordonna called after him.

This meant he could eat pretty well anything except burgers and chips, but then he would never eat food like that anyway, even if it had clotted blood poured over it. He could still remember how sick he had been when he had eaten a sausage covered in coagulated blood, only to discover it wasn't blood but tomato sauce. He hadn't been able to put anything red in his mouth for days.

Like most places in Port Folio after midnight, the undertakers' building just down the road from the hotel was deserted. All the doors were locked and the lights were out. Even the dustbins round the back were secure behind a tall wire fence. Of course, Valla could have changed himself into a bat and flown over the fence, but it took a lot of energy changing back and forth between creatures and Valla's nose told him there was nothing in the

dustbin worth salvaging. You might think this meant that Valla had a brilliant sense of smell, but he didn't. Instead he pulled his nose off, pushed it through the fence and watched as it wriggled up the side of the bin like a big white slug. It wriggled under the lid and two minutes later came back. Valla stuck it back on his face and took a big sniff.

There was nothing, not even a scab or two, just old teabags and rubbish.

The other undertakers' building, at the poorer end of town away from the beach, was not so neat and tidy. Sure, it was all locked up and dark, but its dustbins were just standing in the alley outside the back door. Valla didn't need to take his nose off to check them out. He didn't even need to lift the lids to know there was treasure there. Its delicate aroma greeted him as soon as he turned into the dark alley. And sure enough both bins were like a fine restaurant, a regular vampire's delicatessen.

The first bin yielded up three fingers and a pair of very hairy nostrils. The second one held the jackpot – an entire foot. Valla collected all the body bits in his environmentally biodegradable non-toxic shopping bag and carried them up to the graveyard, which stood on a small hill behind the town.

As he sat leaning against the gravestone of Mildred Flambard 1783–1803, picking the nasal hairs from between his teeth, he looked out across the town and felt completely at peace with the world. The moon shone across the calm sea. Here

and there a few lights twinkled and a small fishing boat chugged out of the harbour on the early tide.

Life doesn't get much better than this, he thought as he finished the last of his takeaway snack.

He was about to nod off to sleep when he heard a tapping directly beneath him. As he stood up, the big stone slab he had been sitting on slid aside and a thin arm came up out of the grave.

'Oww, ahh, ooh,' said a voice from inside the grave.

'Hello?' said Valla.

'Oh,' said the voice. 'I did not realise there was someone there. I do not suppose you could give me a hand, could you? This slab is very heavy. I have been trying to move it every night for . . . umm, pray tell me, what is the year?'

'It's two thousand and eight,' said Valla.

'Mercy me,' said the voice. 'I have been trying to move this slab for two hundred and five years.'

'You mean, you've never been able to in all that time?' said Valla, intrigued.

'No,' said the voice. 'I am but a frail woman.'

Valla pushed the slab aside and the thin arm was joined by a thin body. Valla reached down, took the hand and helped the body climb out onto the grass.

'Mildred Flambard, I presume,' he said.

'Indeed so,' said Mildred. 'Please do not be frightened.'

'I'm not,' said Valla, hypnotised by a creature that looked as if it had been dead for years, but was actually still alive.

Sort of.

Mildred's beauty was the sort of beauty men can only dream of. For normal men, and even for most wizards, that dream would be a terrifying nightmare, but for Valla it was a dream of perfection, a dream that filled his head with but one thought – *death doesn't get any better than this*.

'People are usually petrified,' said Mildred. 'I do not know why, but the living just do not seem to be able to handle the dead talking to them.'

'Look at me,' said Valla. 'Do I look like people?'

'No, not exactly,' said Mildred. 'You look as I do. Oh I see, you are dead. Did you just die recently?'

'I'm not dead,' said Valla, feeling very flattered that Mildred thought he was. 'I'm a wizard.'

'Really?' said Mildred. 'Well, I must say, you are the most handsome wizard I have ever seen and I have seen four of them.'

Valla blushed, which in his case meant turning even whiter.

'In fact,' Mildred added, fluttering her eyelids, 'one could say you are drop-dead gorgeous.'

Valla was speechless. He was in love. Here was a girl with so much sophistication that she even knew the drop-dead gorgeous joke. Here was a girl that he could take home to his parents, a girl he knew they would thoroughly approve of.

'Tell me,' he said. He took Mildred's hand in his, then – realising that he was so deeply in love with her that he had no desire to eat it, despite it looking incredibly delicious – he gave it back to her. 'Tell me. How did you die so young?'

Mildred hesitated, as if unsure what to say.

'I had the plague and the ostrich pox[46] and I was poisoned by a young man who I rejected and I got trampled by a runaway horse while crossing the street to the pharmacy to collect medicine for

---

[46] *Ostrich pox is like chicken pox only with MUCH bigger spots.*

my tuberculosis,' she said. 'I suppose it was just my time to go.'

'How romantic,' said Valla, rejecting the idea of nibbling on Mildred's ear in case he ended up eating all of her.

'I have lain these past two centuries and more waiting for my true love to arrive,' said Mildred. 'And here you are, my Prince Charming.'

As the moon sank over the horizon and the first rays of sunshine tip-toed over the mountain top behind them, Mildred Flambard dropped back into her grave and Valla slid her stone slab over her.[47]

'Fear not, my darling,' Valla said as he slid the stone back the last few millimetres. 'I am from a family of wizards and I am sure that you and I are bound together by destiny. My family has access to all the magic of the universe and I will work out a way to free you forever from your tomb of darkness.'

---

[47] *Because, as everyone knows, if one tiny beam of daylight lands on the living dead, they instantly turn to dust.*

155

And if we can't, Valla thought as he walked back to the hotel, *it's a very nice tomb of darkness with more than enough room for both of us. I'll just move in there.*

When Valla arrived back at the hotel, the family barely recognised him. He was smiling. At least, that was what he said he was doing. If he smiled like that at a baby it would have nightmares.

'You are sure that's what you're doing, aren't you?' said Mordonna.

'I think so,' said Valla. 'I've never smiled before.'

'Well, if you are,' said Merlinmary, 'that's your emo image done for.'

'Oh, I don't know,' said Satanella. 'I think he looks even more depressing.'

'Well, I am not depressed,' said Valla. 'I am in love and we are going to get married.'

He told them all about Mildred and then asked Winchflat if he had a machine or something that could bring her back to as near a state of being alive as possible.

'Tricky,' said Winchflat, 'Of course, there is a very simple solution, but it's not ideal.'

'What's that?'

'Well, if I'm not mistaken, this daylight-into-dust thing only works when the light lands on the corpse's head. I think anywhere else it's harmless. So the obvious thing would be for your girlfriend to wear a big paper bag on her head during the day.'

'Yeah,' laughed Morbid, 'like yours does.'

'Are you sure about the daylight thing?' said Valla. 'Sounds a bit risky.'

'No, I'm not completely sure,' said Winchflat. 'I think it works with some undead creatures, but not with others.'

'I think it's too risky, darling,' said Mordonna. 'I mean, it could all go horribly wrong and you could end up with a head in a bag and a pile of dust.'

'OK,' said Winchflat. 'I'll think of something else.'

'Couldn't you turn her into a zombie, Mother?' asked Valla. 'Or just clone her?'

'Cloning could work,' said Winchflat. 'We could take one of her cells and use the special photocopier at school to copy it until we had enough cells to make a whole Mildred Flambard.'

'Have you ever done anything like that before?' said Mordonna. 'It sounds terribly complicated.'

'I've done it with an omelette, but not with a human being,' said Winchflat. 'I've always wanted to try it, though.'

'It sounds like it could take a very long time,' said Valla.

'Yes. I'll have to work it out,' said Winchflat. 'A human body has about thirty-five trillion cells. So first of all I would photocopy one cell and then photocopy that one and the original together so we got two, and then copy those so we got four and so on. It could take a while. The omelette took seven months and . . . well, there were a few problems.'

'Problems?'

'Yes, it turned out with five legs and ran away,' said Winchflat. 'I never saw it again, though I heard a rumour it was living in the Amazon rainforest with a raggle-taggle group of other egg-based beings calling themselves the Omelette Liberation Front.'

'Er, let's forget the cloning plan,' said Valla.

'So it's down to zombification or simply bringing her back to life then,' said Betty.

'Looks like it,' said Winchflat, who didn't really fancy either option because they were things his mother would do and not him, and it meant he wouldn't have an excuse to invent yet another brilliant machine. 'Unless we used my Massive-Electric-Shock-Dead-Person-iReviver,[48] though I've only ever used that on bodies that have just died, not on two-hundred-year-old corpses with bits missing.'

They couldn't decide between living or zombie, and when Valla tossed a coin it didn't help

---

[48] *See the back of* The Floods 1: Neighbours.

either because the window was open and the coin flew out into the street and fell down a drain.[49]

'When you go to meet your beloved tonight, darling, I will come with you,' said Mordonna. 'We will let her decide.'

As soon as Valla pushed the stone slab aside and Mordonna saw Mildred Flambard, she knew that the girl was the perfect match for her son. Her pale grey skin and sunken eyes were a lovely contrast to his pale grey skin and sunken eyes. The two of them were so alike that they could have been brother and sister, except Mildred Flambard said she had not had a brother and Valla looked nothing like any of his siblings.

'You look so beautiful together,' said Mordonna with a tear in her eye. 'So now, Mildred, you must

---

[49] *Incredibly, the coin landed heads-side up at the foot of a sewer rat, Wick Dittington, who was trying to decide whether to stay in the drains of Port Folio or go away to the big city to seek fame and fortune and more fame tinged with a bit of exciting scandal. This, of course, is another fascinating story, but suffice it to say, the rat not only achieved fortune and fame, but became Lord Mayor of London.*

decide: living or zombie? I can do either.'

'If I am not mistaken, Mother,' said Valla, blushing, 'zombies cannot have babies, can they?'

'You're absolutely right,' said Mordonna. 'Then I shall bring Mildred back to the land of the living.'

'And I shall live and breathe again as I did before I caught the plague and the pox and TB and Curse of the Newt?' said Mildred.

'Yes, my dear,' said Mordonna. 'You will be perfect, as is my firstborn, your husband-to-be, my gorgeous Valla.'

'But my sweetheart won't be all glowing and rosy-cheeked and horribly fit and healthy-looking, will she?' said Valla. 'She will still be the same staggeringly beautiful, ghostly living corpse, won't she?'

'Well, or course, my darling,' said Mordonna. 'I will perform a cocktail of spells. The first will turn her into a zombie. Then I will do the De-Zombify spell and finally I will do the Collect-Up-All-The-Bits-That-Have-Fallen-Off spell so your bride-to-be has all her bits and pieces in proper working order.'

'I'll still be able to howl at the moon, won't I?'

said Mildred. 'I used to love howling before I died.'

'You used to howl at the moon when you were alive?' said Mordonna, suddenly sounding very, very excited.

'Yes,' said Mildred. 'Does that matter?'

'Matter? Oh my goodness no,' said Mordonna, 'quite the opposite. How did you say you died?'

'Umm, I, er, umm, the plague, umm, runaway horse . . .' Mildred began.

'But that's not true, is it?'

'No,' said Mildred. 'I was burnt at the stake as a witch.'

'Did they do all the medieval witch tests on you while you kept denying it?' said Mordonna.

Mildred Flambard nodded and hung her head.

'But they were right, weren't they? You are a witch, aren't you?' said Mordonna.

Mildred Flambard nodded again. 'Does this mean you will not restore me to life?' she asked.

'Oh no, my dear,' said Mordonna. 'It means

you are even more perfect than we thought you were. Come here and give your mother-in-law-to-be a hug, then we will begin.'

The new moon was only three days old, but it was simply a matter of a quick spell to turn it into a full moon, which is the best sort of moon under which to perform spells to bring people back to life. The whole world and everything in it was bathed in an eerie blue light.

Mildred Flambard lay stretched out on the moss-covered slab of the grave that had been her home and prison for the last two hundred and five years, as Mordonna began to chant in a deep prehistoric moan that sent shivers down the spines of all those who heard it.[50]

'Keep your voice down, Mother,' Valla hissed. 'We're in a graveyard and there's no knowing who or what is in some of these tombs. You could wake up a whole army of horrors that might invade the town.'

---

[50] *Except hedgehogs and echidnas.*

'Well, that would make it a lot more lively, wouldn't it, darling,' Mordonna laughed. 'But you don't need to worry. These spells are tailored to work only on your beloved and no one else. Her DNA will act like a PIN so no one else can use the magic.'

Thirteen owls and seventy-seven bats gathered in the trees around the graveyard as Mordonna's chanting reached its highest pitch.

There was a flash of light, a cloud of white smoke and Mildred Flambard sat bolt upright, as alive as she had been the day she died. Or rather, as alive as she had been the day *before* she had died. At the exact same moment, the thirteen owls turned into bats. The seventy-seven bats turned into owls and, five streets away, a car turned into a side street. Also, though no one saw it or even knew, every single corpse and skeleton in the other ninety-three graves sighed and turned over.

'All we have to do now,' said Mordonna as they walked back to the hotel, 'is get you two married.'

'And maybe Winchflat could give you a two-

hundred-year service – changing all your blood, oiling your bones and cleaning out your ears with a toothbrush dipped in bleach,'[51] said Valla as he opened the door to the hotel suite.

'I'd be delighted to, and I think I speak for all of us when I say welcome to our family,' said Winchflat.

Getting married for wizards is entirely different than it is for humans, especially when one of the wizards has been dead for as long as Mildred Flambard. For a start, it is extremely dangerous to kiss someone who has been dead that long because their lips could well end up stuck to yours, not in a romantic

love story Their-Lips-Locked sort of way, but in a Stuck-On-Your-Face-After-They-Have-Left-The-Room sort of way. Also because of the huge amounts of static electricity and nuclear fission that can be generated when wizards fall in love, it is essential for the bride to wear a dress made of lead. Being so long near-dead, Mildred was not strong enough to carry the weight of a lead dress, so to be on the safe side, Valla went into one room, Mildred into another and they were married by email.[52]

---

[52] *Humans never get married by email because they think it isn't very romantic. Humans do, however, split up and get divorced by email — something wizards never do.*

*A*lthough they all went to the beach pretty well every day, Mordonna and Nerlin preferred it at night. At two in the morning it was always deserted, the only sound the gentle splashing of the waves collapsing on the beach. If they went out and there was a wild wind blowing, making the sea noisy and throwing sand into your face, it was only a matter of a couple of quick spells for the wind to creep away and grow lazy again. If there were clouds across the sky, another spell sent them off to Belgium.

There was something about the cold blue moon shining on the night-time sea that made them feel very relaxed and romantic. The children

were back in the hotel. The Hulberts were tucked up in their beds and Queen Scratchrot was quietly disintegrating in her backpack in Winchflat's wardrobe. It was a peaceful time, when the world was nearly asleep.

On the last night of their holiday, as they were moon-bathing on the beach, the ground wobbled beneath them.

'What was that?' said Mordonna.

'Sorry,' said Nerlin. 'Must have been something I ate.'

'No, not that,' said Mordonna. 'That wobble. It wasn't here. It was miles away. It felt like the world had hiccups.'

'If you asked me to guess,' said Nerlin, 'I would say that a new volcano has just erupted at the bottom of the deepest part of the ocean. But then it could just be my imagination.'

'OH MY GOD, THE MARIANA TRENCH!' cried Mordonna, sitting bolt upright and staring out to sea.

'Yes, that's the place,' said Nerlin.

'Oh no,' said Mordonna.

'What's the matter?' said Nerlin.

'That's where the Hearse Whisperer is,' said Mordonna. 'Don't you remember? The children and I lured her into a magic bottle, sealed it shut and buried it at the bottom of the Mariana Trench. We thought it would be most secure place on earth.'[53]

'Well, if it's a magic bottle,' said Nerlin, 'I'm sure there's nothing to worry about. All the hot lava has probably sucked it right into the core of the planet where nothing could survive.'

'The Hearse Whisperer is fireproof,' said Mordonna. 'Even her underwear can withstand the strongest furnace. Her knickers are made of the same stuff they stick on the outside of the space shuttle, only without any holes or torn bits.'

'But surely no living creature could survive boiling lava?' said Nerlin.

---

[53] *To find out ALL about this, see* The Floods 5: Prime Suspect.

'I suppose not,' said Mordonna, though she still looked doubtful.

Something dark staggered out of the water, a huge, menacing silhouette against the moonlit ocean.

The two wizards sat immobile.

Was this the end?

After all their hiding, had the Hearse Whisperer finally found them?

'Hello, Mum,' it said. 'Thanks for that.'

It was Winchflat. The earthquake had shaken him free from the sand.

'Winchflat, what are you doing going back in the sea when you got stuck the first time?' said Mordonna.

'Er, umm, nothing, Mum,' said Winchflat, blushing inside his diving helmet.

He had gone back because, like his mother, he couldn't believe one of his inventions hadn't worked properly. Failure was NOT his middle name and he was determined to have another go at this swimming thing.

'Anyway, that wobble wasn't me, darling,' said Mordonna. 'It was an earthquake.'

'Uh oh,' said Winchflat. 'Bet it was in the Mariana Trench. You know, I thought this might happen, but I didn't say anything. I mean, the odds against it were twenty-three billion and fifty-seven to one against it happening, so it didn't seem very likely, except that twenty-three billion and fifty-seven is the mysterious da Vinci number that has

been linked to a whole series of weird, unexplained events over the past four hundred and fifty years.'

'Come on, stop worrying, said Nerlin. 'Say the very worst happens and the Hearse Whisperer does escape – she still doesn't know where we live.'

'That's true, but she's going to be in a really bad mood,' said Mordonna. 'I don't mean the really bad mood that she's in all the time. I mean the incredibly, unbelievably, horribly bad mood that would make her melt babies and tie angelfish in knots before deep-frying them for lunch.'

'Yes, yes, but she still doesn't know how to find us,' said Nerlin. 'I mean, she couldn't find us before, so what makes you think she can now?'

'I suppose so, but I still have this terrible uneasy feeling,' she said as they walked back to the hotel for a cup of cocoa.

'You are such a worrier, Mum,' said Betty at breakfast the next morning. 'A bit of an earth tremor and you think the worst.'

. . . And a massive earthquake occurred last night deep in the Pacific Ocean's Mariana Trench, measuring seventeen point two on the Richter Scale, said a voice on the hotel dining room radio, *leading to the creation of a completely new island that is now towering over the other fourteen islands in the Marianas . . .*

'See, I told you,' said Mordonna.

'Tears before bedtime,' said the Queen from her backpack under the table. 'I can sense it. Have I ever told you that I have an unerring ability to sense impending doom?'

'Yes, all the time,' chorused everyone, including the waiter.

Mordonna said she thought they should leave as soon as possible, but the others suggested that there wasn't much point because if the Hearse Whisperer was going to find them, she had as

174

much or as little chance of doing so in Port Folio as anywhere else.

'So seeing as how everywhere is as safe as everywhere else, we might as well stay here,' said Winchflat.

'Did you bring your Hearse-Whisperer-Early-Warning-Device?' said Betty when they had all gone back upstairs.

'No, I'm afraid I left it in Acacia Avenue,' said Winchflat. 'I'll just have to rely on the detector hairs in my nose. They don't have the range of my machine, but it's better than nothing.'

'Couldn't you send a signal to Igorina and get her to use the device?'

'Well, I can send her a signal, no problem,' said Winchflat. 'But I have a hard enough time trying to get her to use the toilet, never mind a complicated piece of equipment. Still, I suppose it's worth a try.'

He switched on his communicator and hunched over the tiny screen, fiddling with the controls.

'That's strange,' he said. 'I don't seem to be able to make contact.'

Instead of showing the padded cell at 13 Acacia Avenue that Igorina called home,[54] the screen was just a dark swirling mass, like a thunderstorm without the storm or the thunder.

'That looks like the weather outside,' said Betty.

Outside the hotel windows, the sky had become as black as night, even though it was only ten o'clock in the morning.

'This is not good,' said Mordonna.

The uneasy feeling she had when the deep sea volcano had erupted now advanced past uneasy and on to really scary and needing a cup of very strong tea.

'You're absolutely right,' said Queen Scratchrot. 'The impending doom hairs on the back of my neck are wriggling like crazy. I would say that it's all systems go on impending doom.'

---

[54] *Igorina didn't actually call her padded cell home, she called it 'unghh', which was basically what she called everything.*

'It's just a storm,' said Nerlin. 'You women are such worriers.'

'Those are the exact words that the theatre manager in Silly said to me the night my beloved died,' said the Queen. 'And look how that ended.'

A great wind began to blow and behind the hills at the back of Port Folio, far away in the distance in the exact direction of the town where Acacia Avenue was, ferocious flashes of lightning lit up the sky with no gaps between them.

'This is very not good,' said Mordonna. 'This will end in tears long, long before bedtime.'

'See,' said the Queen, 'told you so.'

'The screen on my Keep-An-Eye-On-Things-At-Home-Scanner has gone dead,' said Winchflat. 'And my Keep-An-Eye-On-My-Keep-An-Eye-On-Things-At-Home-Scanner-Scanner is dead too.'

As the whole family waited and worried on the top floor of the Hotel Splendide, Winchflat tapped the screens on his receivers and they all showed the same thing.

Nothing.

'What about your Keep-An-Eye-On-Your-Keep-An-Eye-On-Your-Keep-An-Eye-On-Things-At-Home-Scanner-Scanner-Scanner?' said Betty, who knew just how well prepared her brother always was.

'Dead too,' said Winchflat, facing the terrible prospect of another invention failure, 'and so is the backup and the backup-backup.'

Of course, what Winchflat didn't realise was that all his machines were working perfectly. The 'nothing' they could see was not nothing. It was thick black smoke that looked exactly like nothing.

'I don't want to alarm anyone, but I can smell smoke,' said Satanella, who, being a dog, had a sense of smell a hundred times more sensitive than human noses and thirty-seven times better than a wizard.

Ruby and Rosie weren't worried. They were Jack Russells, and Jack Russells don't believe in worrying. Ruby and Rosie were running around the hotel biting holes in all the pairs

of shoes people had left outside their doors for polishing.

Twelve floors meant eighty-seven pairs of shoes, all demanding to be chewed, run around with, tossed down the stairs and muddled up.

When Mordonna had rescued the two little dogs from the pound and brought them back to the hotel, she had given them the power of speech on the strict condition that they were never to use it when there were any humans around – except in extreme emergencies.

'You know what?' said Ruby as she tore the heel off a really, really expensive Manolo Blahnik shoe.

'What?' said Rosie as she bit a row of holes in a pair of handmade waterproof boots.

'Life doesn't get any better than this!'

'Right on, sister,' said Rosie. 'Let's go down to the laundry and eat some undies.'

The wind lifted half the sand off the beach and threw it at Belgium. Only Betty and Ffiona's castle remained untouched, though the trained hermit

crabs inside all ran and hid under the miniature beds.

'It's the Hearse Whisperer,' said Mordonna. 'I know it is. She's escaped from the magic bottle and is taking it out on the whole world.'

'Don't worry,' said Nerlin. 'There's no way she can find us. We just have to sit tight and wait until she calms down again.'

'The Hearse Whisperer is never calm,' said Mordonna. 'If she has to kill everyone in the whole country to find us, she'll do it.'

'Relax, Mother,' said Valla. 'She doesn't even know which country we are in.'

Winchflat went very white, which was actually an improvement on his normal grey-with-green-and-maroon-streaks colour.

'What is it?' said Mordonna.

'She can find us,' he said. 'We left her a clue.'

'What?' said Mordonna. 'How . . .? Why . . .? I mean, you're always so careful.'

'Well, we didn't think she'd ever, ever be able to escape,' said Winchflat. 'After we had trapped

her in the bottle on that little island in Tristan da Cunha, I put the bottle in a padded envelope to stop it getting broken while we sent it down to the bottom of the sea.'

'And you left the padded envelope down there, didn't you?' said Morbid.

'Yes,' said Winchflat. 'And because it was an enchanted bottle, it wouldn't have got broken anyway so we didn't even need the envelope.'

'Hang on a minute,' said Valla. 'Was it the envelope I got the free blood samples sent from Paraguay in?'

'Yes.'

'Which had our address on it?'

'Yes,' said Winchflat, sounding miserable.

Everyone cursed at once with every single swear word they had ever heard.

'It'll be all right,' said Betty. 'There's nine of us and only one of her, and we trapped her once, we can do it again.'

'And we're not at home,' said Nerlin cheerfully. 'So that's all right.'

Before Mordonna could say anything, something came flying in through the window. The window was shut at the time, so the something flew into the window, smashed the glass with an almighty crash, and then came flying through it. It landed in a heap on the floor.

It was Parsnip.

'Big panic doing,' he croaked and fainted.

Mordonna picked up the unconscious bird and tucked him inside her cloak. Soon the warmth of the witch's body revived him and after a snack of dead mackerel he was back to being as normal as a Transylvanian Crow ever is.

'Flee doing now,' he said. 'Acacia Avenue charcoal being.'

'What?'

'Fire, Worse Hisperer playing with matches done. Boom, boom. All gone.'

'All gone?' said Mordonna.

'Huge deep hole, big flame. Snip-Snip even lost dead pigeon dinner,' said Parsnip.

'What about *our* house?' said Ffiona, who had come rushing in to see what the crashing sound was.

'Think all right, just thirteen and eleven gone. Snip-Snip not see nineteen in big smoke.'

'Are we in danger?' said Mrs Hulbert when Mordonna explained to her what had happened.

Since she had had her beauty treatment that

183

morning, Mrs Hulbert had been floating around the hotel feeling very, very relaxed. In fact she had spent the past few hours on Planet Relaxed, which meant she had been completely unaware of the storm raging outside. She had been lying on her bed drinking champagne and eating chocolates while hippy music floated through her head. She had been idly wondering if she should become a hippy too, and spend the rest of her life in a field full of pretty flowers. The news that large parts of Acacia Avenue, possibly including her own home, had been destroyed, was taking a while to sink in. Mrs Hulbert had more important things to think about, like how soft her skin was and exactly what type of flowers she should grow in her hippy field. It wasn't until baby Claude realised something strange was going on and bit her on the ankle that she came abruptly back to reality, where all the fields were full of potatoes, without a single flower in sight, not even dandelions.

'Are we in danger?' she repeated.

'You've got nothing to worry about,' said

Mordonna. 'The Hearse Whisperer isn't after you. She won't know you have anything to do with us. So if you leave the minibus here and hire a little car just big enough for the four of you and go home, you should be fine. She won't know we've been on holiday. She probably thinks we've just gone shopping.'

'What about my poor Igorina?' said Winchflat.

'Oh yes, I'd forgotten about her, sweetheart,' said Mordonna. 'Correct me if I'm wrong, but you did manufacture her out of readily available parts, didn't you?'

'Well, yes,' said Winchflat. 'But she was a living, breathing creature with a soul.'

'Actually, sweetheart, she was a zombie and, as you know, the only soles zombies have are on the bottom of their feet.'

'But, but . . . we were engaged,' Winchflat said.

'Really?'

'Well, not exactly. I hadn't got round to asking

her, but I'm sure she would have said yes, once I had taught her to speak properly.'

'Never mind, darling,' said Mordonna trying to hide her relief that her son's hideous creation was not going to become her daughter-in-law. 'Parsnip, do you know what happened to my faithful pet vulture, Leach?'

'Him toast become,' said Parsnip. 'Burnt to a crips.'

'A crisp?'

'Yes,' said Parsnip. 'Vulture flavoured crips, him delicious, yum, yum, thank you, better than salt-n-vinegar, better than igorinaflavour.'

'You ate them?' said Mordonna.

'Waste not want not,' said Parsnip. 'Long flying here needed something for journey.'

'Fair enough.'

Winchflat went and sat by the window. Along the beach a team of scientists were still poking and prodding at the turrets of the girls' sandcastle with a whole barrage of high-tech equipment.

Winchflat concentrated hard. The ground

around the sandcastle began to shake. The scientists dropped their equipment and ran. As they did so the entire castle rose slowly into the air. When it was a hundred metres above the beach, there was a blinding flash and fourteen thousand very dead slimy jellyfish came raining down on everyone.

'I thought that would make me feel better,' said Winchflat, 'but it didn't.'

'Never mind, darling,' said Mordonna. 'Why don't you think of poor Igorina as a kind of prototype and when we get settled again you can build a new and much better one.'

'Yeah, one without the pooey smell,' said Morbid.

'Yes,' said Betty, 'one where none of the bits keep falling off.'

'I suppose so,' said Winchflat, 'but you know, no one's ever quite the same as your first love.'

'Actually, I don't, darling,' said Mordonna. 'Your father was my first love, but he is also my last love.'

'Aww,' said Betty.

'Yeughh,' said Merlinmary. 'Sloppy, sloppy.'

'But what are you all going to do?' said Mrs Hulbert.

'We will have to go far, far away,' said Mordonna.

'But, but . . .' Mrs Hulbert began, her bottom lip quivering and tears coming into her eyes. 'You're my best friend, Mordonna. Does this mean I'll never see you again?'

'Of course not,' Mordonna lied. 'Once we get somewhere safe, we'll let you know and you can come and visit us.'

She knew that this would be impossible. The Hearse Whisperer was not stupid. She would probably suspect that the Floods would have made friends in the neighbourhood. So she would be watching everyone in the street. She would hide microscopic tracking devices under the skin behind the left knee of every man, woman and child in Acacia Avenue while they were asleep. She would even tag the dogs and cats. She would know where every single one of them was all the time. Mordonna

knew that no matter how safe and secure their eventual hiding place would be, they would never be able to see the Hulberts again.

Betty knew this too and wrapped Ffiona up in her arms and hugged her tight until Ffiona realised it as well. The two of them went to Ffiona's room and, while she packed her bag, Betty tried to reassure her.

'Look, we're witches and wizards,' she said. 'We are the cleverest people in the world, and there are nine of us – nine-and-a-half if you count Granny – and there is only one Hearse Whisperer. I know she's evil and cunning, but we caught her once before, so I'm sure we can do it again. And then you can come and see us, or we could even come back and build a new house in Acacia Avenue.'

'OK,' said Ffiona, unconvinced.

All she could see was that without Betty to look after her at school, there was a strong possibility that having her head flushed down the toilet might start all over again. She'd be able to pretend that Betty was just on an extended holiday and coming back any minute, but eventually the bullies would work it out and her life would become sheer misery.

'And don't worry about the school bullies,' said Betty. 'I'll get Mum to cast an invincible protection spell over you so that if anyone comes within a metre of you planning to do something horrible, they will have instant toothache and terrible diarrhoea.'

Ffiona looked up hopefully at Betty.

'So if the bullies start taunting you from across the street, all you have to do is the exact opposite of what they expect you to do,' Betty added.

'How do you mean?'

'Well, they'll be expecting you to run away, won't they?'

'I suppose so,' said Ffiona.

'But what you do is run straight at them and, as soon as you get to within one metre of them, bam – screaming headache and runny bottom. Them, that is, not you,' said Betty. 'And if a teacher or anyone else is being mean to you, you can do it to them too.'

The two girls returned to the living room, where the Hulberts were waiting with their luggage. Betty turned to Satanella. 'One other thing,' she said. 'I think that Ruby and Rosie should go with the Hulberts. We might be running away a fair bit and hiding and moving around a lot and . . . well, Claude adores them. But Satanella, they're your friends so you should decide.'

'I adore them too,' said Satanella, 'but I agree, they'll be safer and happier with the Hulberts.' She ran off to say goodbye to her friends.

'But I will see you again, won't I?' said Ffiona.

'I promise you that one day we will see each other again,' said Betty. 'And a witch's promise is the most powerful promise you can get.'

EPILOGUE

There isn't one. I mean, the story isn't over yet.

The Floods haven't even had their blood-red slurpies like they did at the end of the first five Floods books. But since they don't have a verandah to sit and drink them on any more, we'd better let them drive off into the sunset, until they find a new home in the next book.[55]

---

[55] *Or the one after that.*

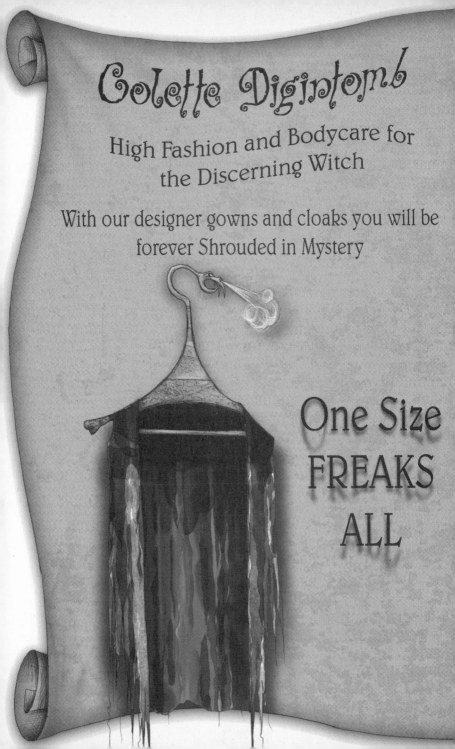

Do you want skin like sun-bleached bones?

Well, of course you do.

Why should Emos and Goths be the only ones looking as though they died a week ago?

SIMPLY buy yourself a barrel of **Super Blockout with added Sulphuric Acid** for that gorgeous textured look.

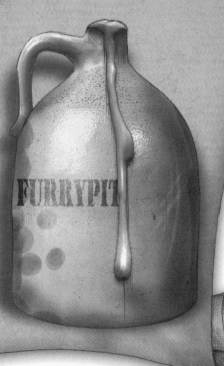

UNSIGHTLY BODY HAIR? Grow inches more OVERNIGHT With FURRYPIT!

THE DEAD-GRANNY BACKPACK

MODEL 1: Basic - $237 + 2 litres Blood
MODEL 2: De-Luxe - $432 + 3 litres Blood

The De-Luxe model includes a slime collector and drip tray, Festerproof lining and soundproofing.

Dead Granny not included, though we do have them for sale from time to time.

Available from:
STIFF SHOULDERS,
BO Box 27,
Decay Street,
Gastown,
TRANSYLVANIA
WATERS OMG34

IF you don't have a dead granny to put in your backpack, then one of these might come in handy.

You'll also need one of these because people get annoyed when you dig up dead bodies. I don't know why. If they are so special, why do people bury them in the first place?

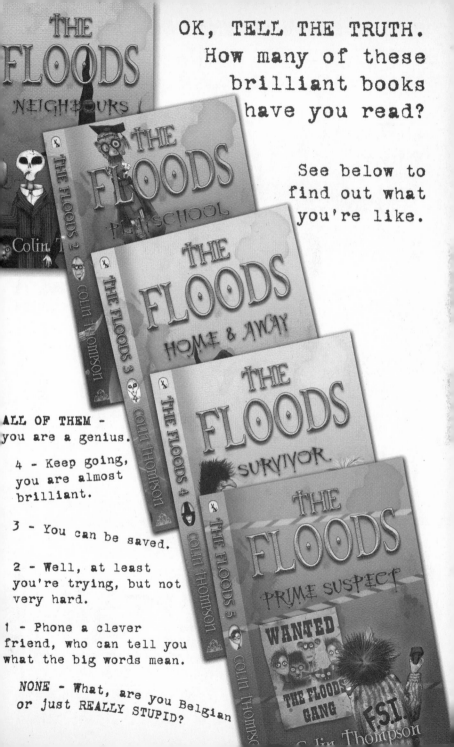

OK, TELL THE TRUTH.
How many of these
brilliant books
have you read?

See below to
find out what
you're like.

ALL OF THEM -
you are a genius.

4 - Keep going,
you are almost
brilliant.

3 - You can be saved.

2 - Well, at least
you're trying, but not
very hard.

1 - Phone a clever
friend, who can tell you
what the big words mean.

NONE - What, are you Belgian
or just REALLY STUPID?

AND, of course, don't forget to TOTALLY
INCREASE your FLOODS ENJOYMENT by reading
this HUGE, FULL COLOUR picture book

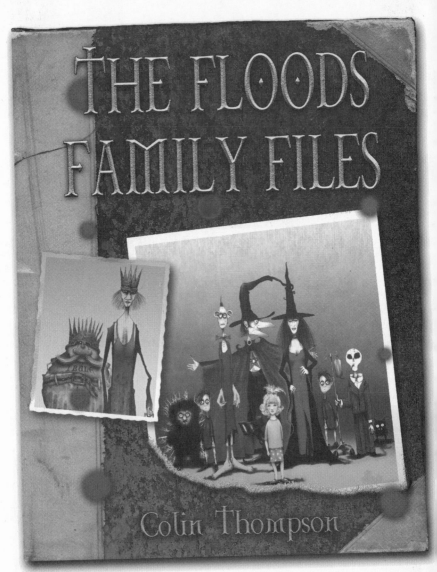

In ALL GOOD bookshops now and even in
some BAD, WICKED and NASTY ones too.

Promise me that, no matter what happens, no matter how desperate you feel, no matter who asks you, you will never, never, never, read this book.

Hidden behind the hundreds of secret doors in the museum, Peter will find an enchanted world, a cursed book and a terrible choice that could change his life for eternity.

HOW TO LIVE FOREVER

Colin Thompson

AVAILABLE NOW AT ALL GOOD BOOKSTORES.

COMING in 2009 - Book 2
The Second Forever

RANDOM HOUSE AUSTRALIA
www.randomhouse.com.au